ROSAMUNDE
WANTED TO REMAIN STRONG
IN LORD MERRITT'S PRESENCE . . .

Yet she found she needed to rest her back against the wall to keep from collapsing.

"Miss Wickes. Rosamunde," Lord Merritt said softly. He lifted his hand to her shoulder as he moved to stand before her. "Did they harm you?"

He placed his other hand upon her arm. He ran his hands up and down her arms, slowly, as if searching for injuries. She knew Raikes and Gidley had not harmed her—not yet—but the pounding of her own heart at Lord Merritt's gentle touch made her breast ache.

"They . . . they want to know where the treasure is. They threatened . . ."

"I am so glad you are safe," he said.

"I'm glad you were here . . ."

"I want to keep you safe, Rosamunde."

He stepped closer to her.

She felt his breath upon her cheek, warm and sweet. Slowly, he lowered his face until his lips touched hers, softly, gently.

A Love To Treasure

Melinda Pryce

DIAMOND BOOKS, NEW YORK

A LOVE TO TREASURE

A Diamond Book / published by arrangement with
the author

PRINTING HISTORY
Diamond edition / March 1992

ISBN: 1-55773-677-4

Diamond Books are published by The Berkley Publishing Group,
200 Madison Avenue, New York, New York 10016.
The name "DIAMOND" and its logo are trademarks
belonging to Charter Communications, Inc.

PRINTED IN THE UNITED STATES OF AMERICA

10 9 8 7 6 5 4 3 2 1

In loving memory of
Frederick H. Kreisel
(1924–1990)
My Dad, My First Hero

=ONE=

"Hoist the mainsail! Keelhaul the first mate!" Sir Polly ordered.

The vicar's teacup rattled in its saucer.

"More milk for your tea, Mr. Shelby?" Mrs. Wickes asked politely. She pointedly refused even to look in Sir Polly's direction, thus signifying her blatant refusal to comply with his ludicrous commands.

"More rum, wench!" Sir Polly demanded, indignant at being ignored.

"No, thank you," the visibly shaken Reverend Mr. Shelby responded quickly. He mopped at the splash of tea which spotted his black broadcloth breeches, all the while continuing to mumble, "I find it quite delicious just as it is, thank you. Quite delicious, indeed."

"Belay that bilge, ye lily-livered scum!" Sir Polly commanded.

Mr. Shelby, his round face flushed, immediately ceased speaking.

Mrs. Wickes turned to her stepdaughter, who was seated beside her on the well-worn blue damask sofa. Without even appearing to move her lips, Mrs. Wickes whispered, "Rosamunde, do be a proper hostess and offer Mr. Shelby a clean serviette."

Rosamunde made no reply. For want of more stimulating conversation, she had been mentally wagering with herself. Which of the persons assembled here this afternoon would be the first to cry surrender in the face of the autocratic Sir Polly?

Would it be the Reverend Mr. Josiah Shelby? Rosamunde could easily picture the timid gentleman becoming so unnerved by the outrageous language that he would drop his clumsily held teacup and hastily bid them all adieu.

Would it be her stepmother? Mrs. Wickes was struggling valiantly to maintain a placid demeanor in the vicar's presence, but Rosamunde believed she would soon declare that she had suffered sufficient humiliation and have Sir Polly forcibly removed from the room.

Rosamunde was absolutely certain that it would *not* be her stepsister, fragile-looking, fair-haired Mary Ann. In the seven years since her father had married the widowed Mrs. Catherine Bellows and brought her and her eleven-year-old daughter into their home, Rosamunde had never seen Mary Ann dare to do *anything* first.

'I have long suspected that Mary Ann had an older sibling who died at birth,' Rosamunde silently speculated, 'as I greatly doubt that she would even have enough courage to be firstborn.'

Rosamunde also knew that neither she nor her uncle would leave. They both harbored a great deal of affection for the cantankerous old Sir Polly, and believed that, in his own peculiar way, Sir Polly liked them, too.

"Rosamunde!" Mrs. Wickes repeated with just the tiniest bit more volume while ever so subtly dealing Rosamunde a sharp poke in the ribs with her elbow. "How can you not hear me when you are sitting directly beside me?"

"Oh!" Rosamunde started at the jab. She made certain this time to turn her left ear to her stepmother. "I beg your pardon. I fear I was woolgathering."

"In Mr. Shelby's company?" Mrs. Wickes' voice rose to indicate her disbelief as much as her censure. She shook her head. "Mark my words, no gentleman will continue to call upon a lady who is inattentive to him, much less deign to court such a girl."

After this last remark, Rosamunde fully expected to see the timid vicar bolt for the door like a frightened rabbit for the underbrush. Yet Mr. Shelby calmly reached for another forcemeat sandwich.

In truth, it was not that Rosamunde did not care for the quiet, young vicar. He was an intelligent, well-educated, and well-spoken man. However, with his gently curling brown hair, his saggy jowls, and his doleful brown eyes, he reminded Rosamunde of a roly-poly little hound puppy.

'Except he is taller,' Rosamunde noted to herself with a little grin. 'He does sit better upon the furniture and eat more neatly. Indeed, it is not so much the man himself which puts me off,' she silently acknowledged. 'It is the simple fact that I cannot abide Stepmama seizing every opportunity to throw me at his head.'

"Now, do pass Mr. Shelby a clean serviette," Mrs. Wickes repeated.

Rosamunde lifted a snowy white serviette from the table and passed it to Mary Ann. Mary Ann smiled shyly at the young vicar as she handed it to him.

"I believe you would have less difficulty in attending to our guest's comfort if you had not chosen to place yourself at such a great distance from him," Mrs. Wickes continued to scold.

Before the vicar's arrival, Mrs. Wickes had instructed the girls at great length upon precisely who was to sit where. However, Rosamunde had defiantly stationed herself between her stepmother and her uncle, who was seated in the chair by the fireside—and as far from Mr. Shelby as possible. She had left *that* singular honor to Mary Ann.

Suddenly Sir Polly declared, "A comely wench! Make ready to board, me hearties!"

Mrs. Wicke drew in an audible gasp and clenched her fists in her lap. She turned in exasperation to her brother-in-law, and to his offending companion, who was settled upon his shoulder.

"Oh, I vow, Dudley," she exclaimed to the wizened,

white-haired man sitting by the fire. "I can bear this no longer! If you cannot make that wretched parrot of yours hush, I shall have it disposed of."

'Aha!' Rosamunde declared to herself. The victor of her wager—the Reverend Mr. Shelby. She was surprised. She really had not expected her formidable stepmother to be the first to cry defeat.

"Ye'll not be harming Sir Polly, ye treacherous harridan!" Her uncle's voice reminded Rosamunde of the creaking of the rusty hinges of their garden gate.

The old man leaned toward Mrs. Wickes and thumped the tip of his wooden leg upon the floor. "Or I'll be forced to give ye a taste o' me broadsword . . ." He drew a deep breath and frowned. "Well, just as soon as I find what ye've done with the bloody thing while me back was turned, ye thieving old harpy!"

"Vicious harpy! Vicious harpy!" Sir Polly cried from his perch on the shoulder of the aging gentleman. He flapped his lucent wings of green and red-tipped yellow.

"And don't be calling me Dudley," he ordered in the same rasping voice. "Ye know full well they called me Peg. Peg o' Penzance, the Murderous Marauder, the Scourge o' the Seven Seas—"

"Peg?" Mrs. Wickes spat out scornfully. "What sort of name is that for a gentleman?"

"Well, what sort o' name be *Dudley* for a pirate?" Peg countered, again stomping the tip of his wooden leg into the carpet.

"Don't *do* that!" Mrs. Wickes ordered, indicating his wooden leg with a nod of her head. "You will ruin the carpet!"

Peg gave one extra thump, apparently just for good measure.

Mrs. Wickes clenched her fists until her knuckles turned white. By contrast, her voice was high-pitched and artificially sweet.

"A pirate, indeed. Oh, Dudley, what will Mr. Shelby think of our family if you tell such outrageous tales?"

"Keelhaul the slimy scum!" Sir Polly declared.

"Dudley was a merchant seaman," Mrs. Wickes confided to Mr. Shelby in a rather loud whisper. "He is my husband's younger brother by a scant sixteen months, but the hard life at sea has aged him prematurely—not to mention the fact that when he was but a boy, he suffered quite a shock. He lost a leg."

"I didn't lose it, ye wretched crone," Peg thundered his correction. "They hacked it from me, the bloody, black-hearted butchers."

Mr. Shelby stop in mid-bite. He slowly placed his sandwich upon the edge of his saucer. Mary Ann's face had a decidedly greenish tinge.

"Lost it, indeed!" Peg muttered. "As if I were some absentminded old sot, misplacing body parts as I went about me daily affairs."

Peg's voice rose two octaves in imitation of Mrs. Wickes. "Oh, pray, excuse me, but have you seen my nose lying about? I'm dining with Lord Stablemuck this evening, and it simply would not do to be seen without it!"

Rosamunde giggled softly to herself. She knew very well that no one else would appreciate Uncle Peg's jest.

Mrs. Wickes turned to Mr. Shelby and sighed, a long-suffering smile upon her face. "Even though he can be rather difficult at times, we felt it our duty to take poor Dudley into our home in his declining years."

"How very kind of you," Mr. Shelby said. He had apparently regained his appetite, as he again took up the remainder of the sandwich.

"Yes, it was," Rosamunde agreed. "As a matter of fact, Uncle Peg has been declining now for almost five years."

Mrs. Wickes shot Rosamunde a threatening glare. Then she returned a beaming smile upon the vicar. "I'm afraid he is quite in his dotage. Just because he acquired that silly bird on one of his voyages . . ." Mrs. Wickes punctuated her complaint with a disdainful gesture in Sir Polly's direction.

The parrot flapped his wings and stretched his hooked beak hungrily toward her plump fingers. Mrs. Wickes quickly replaced them in her lap. With a nervous little laugh, she finished, ". . . he actually believes he was once a pirate."

Mr. Shelby raised a single eyebrow. "Fancy that, poor old fellow."

"However, my husband, Rosamunde's father, is extraordinarily sound of body and mind—as is Rosamunde," Mrs. Wickes said with added emphasis. "Oh, such a healthy girl will be an industrious wife and a doting mother to the many children I'm sure Rosamunde will bear."

Rosamunde grimaced. She felt as if she were a brood mare being discussed by two farmers at the crossroads on market day. Would her stepmother next be offering to show the vicar her teeth? Perhaps she should prance about the room a bit to show off her gait, or toss her dark tresses like a mane behind her. With a grin, she resisted the impulse to whinny. Were it not for her own exasperation, she could almost laugh at her stepmother's foolish persistence.

Mr. Shelby made no comment. He only smiled politely and helped himself to another sandwich. Rosamunde wondered if anyone could actually be that obtuse—or even actually be that hungry.

Sir Polly emitted another ear-splitting squawk. "All hands on deck! Now hear this!" He then began what the family knew very well was the first verse of his long litany of profanities.

The vicar's face turned rosy pink. Mrs. Wickes' grew flaming red. The color of Mary Ann's face could not be discerned as she had covered it with both hands. Rosamunde had to admit that she felt her own cheeks growing rather warm as Sir Polly's recitation continued.

Peg's chuckles turned into outright hearty laughter.

"Mary Ann," Mrs. Wickes called in a voice which was not quite loud enough to drown out Sir Polly's lurid cries.

"Do accompany Uncle Dudley and his pet into the garden for some fresh air."

Mary Ann's wide blue eyes peeped over the tops of her fingertips. She glanced back and forth between her mother and Sir Polly, as if trying to decide which of the two she feared the most. For a moment, it appeared as if Sir Polly would win. Then Mary Ann reluctantly rose and slowly approached the still-cursing parrot.

Upon noticing her approach, Sir Polly began to scratch at the air with one long-taloned foot. "No quarter! No prisoners!" he cried.

"Mama, I truly do not think Sir Polly cares to leave . . ."

"Nonsense, child. Now go."

Rosamunde watched her vacillating stepsister with growing frustration. She felt that if she herself did not soon escape her badgering stepmother and the dull company of Mary Ann and the Silent Vicar, she should scream.

She rose and declared, "Please excuse me. Come, Uncle Peg."

She offered her hand to help Peg rise. The soft scuffle of his leather shoe alternated with the thump of his wooden leg as he headed for the large doors which opened out into the garden behind the house.

"Rosamunde," Mrs. Wicke cried after her. "*You* cannot leave. What will Mr. Shelby think? Oh, Rosamunde, wait!"

Rosamunde turned and smiled at her stepmother. "I shall return."

Once out on the brick terrace, she closed her eyes and drew in a great sigh of relief. It was so good to be away from them. Of course, she had every intention of keeping her promise. She *would* return—she had just not been too precise about when.

Rosamunde followed Peg's slow progress to the edge of the terrace, where they would be out of earshot of the others.

Peg learned his back against the stone balustrade. He

lifted his weather-beaten face to the early summer sunlight and drew in a deep breath.

"Ah, to be at sea once again, lass," came the hoarse cry. "To feel the rise and fall o' the deck beneath me feet. To smell the salt sea in the air as it sprays me face. To hear the halyard creaking in the wind . . ."

He coughed and swallowed hard, then coughed again. In a soft, weak voice, he complained, "I vow, this throat of mine . . ."

He sighed as he eased his gaunt form down onto the stone bench beside the balustrade.

"Poor Uncle Peg," Rosamunde replied sympathetically as she sat to his right. "If it pains you so, why do you persist in adding that awful rasping tone to your voice when you speak?"

"Because it do be the voice of a pirate, lass," Peg declared. Then he chuckled and replied in his own normal voice, "And because I know it aggravates Catherine to distraction."

Rosamunde cast her incorrigible old uncle a skeptical glance. "Were you *really* called Peg o' Penzance?"

Peg patted the wide leather strap buckled about his left thigh. Below the knee was a well-padded socket ending in a smoothly turned peg. "What do you think?" he asked.

"I think you insist upon being called Peg to aggravate Stepmama all the more," Rosamunde replied with a grin.

"Catherine believes in sensible names," Peg said. "That is why she gave such a sensible name to her own daughter."

"Sensible is boring," Rosamunde said. "So is Mary Ann."

"Pox-ridden doxy," Sir Polly proclaimed.

"Mary Ann is shy," Peg said as he rose from the bench. He slowly descended the three stone steps which led to the brick garden walk.

"She is *boring*!" Rosamunde insisted. She snatched up her yellow muslin skirts and quickly caught up with Peg.

"When she came to live here, I thought, at last! A sister

with whom to share secrets and adventures." Rosamunde's fine, dark brows drew into a frown. "Instead, I find myself burdened with a girl who hasn't even the courage to break the end of a boiled egg!"

"You must be patient with her," Peg advised.

Rosamunde grimaced. "Be patient. Be sensible. I suppose next you will be advising me to comply with Stepmama's plans and wed the docile Mr. Shelby."

"Bollixy swab!" Sir Polly accused.

Peg shrugged his shoulders. "Well, why not?"

"Uncle Peg!" Rosamunde cried at his traitorous suggestion.

"You're two and twenty, Rosamunde. At your age, you could do worse."

"He is boring, too," she muttered. "Uncle Peg, for five years I have listened to your tales of adventures on the high seas, and I have loved every minute of it. You have only yourself to blame for filling my head with a longing for adventures of my own."

"You believe you shall never have them if you marry Mr. Shelby?"

"Just look at him! Of course not!"

"Do you think there exists a man who would allow you the opportunity for such adventures?"

"Of course not," she replied with a bitter little laugh.

She knew how silly it was for a lady of her age and modest station and *very* meager income to long for adventures. She could never admit, not even to her beloved Uncle Peg, how much the realization that she would never wander beyond her little town grieved her.

Suddenly Sir Polly flapped his wings and cried, "All hands, abandon ship!"

Peg was frowning at the two men who were approaching from the far end of the garden.

"Who are they, Uncle Peg? How dare they enter uninvited?"

"Be a good lass and return to the house," was all Peg answered. "Take Sir Polly with you."

Rosamunde stretched out her arm. Sir Polly stepped his little sideways walk down the green wool of Peg's old jacket, then up the soft yellow muslin of Rosamunde's sleeve. She could feel his talons, like minuscule pinpricks through the fabric, as he circled about. Then he settled comfortably on her shoulder.

The sight of the two men strolling boldly toward her uncle sent a shiver of alarm—and yes, of morbid fascination, too—up her spine to chill the back of her neck.

"I shall summon the constable," she announced with determination, turning to go.

Peg laid a restraining hand on her arm and shook his head. "No need for the constable. I'll come to no harm from those two."

The shorter man removed his battered black hat and, bending low, swept it past his stockings, which were badly in need of mending, and across his equally battered shoes. A tattered cravat dangled down the front of his rusty black velvet coat.

"Mr. Raikes," Peg said in clipped syllables and with only the slightest nod of the head.

"How good to see ye again," Raikes replied. The narrow white scar that ran from his left temple then under his eye and down to the edge of his nose puckered as he smiled. His thin lips drew back, revealing his few remaining, rotting teeth. "And a good day to yer lovely companion," he added, bowing to Rosamunde.

Rosamunde nodded politely.

"What a charming animal that be," Raikes said.

The parrot flapped his wings frantically, but said nothing.

"My niece's pet."

"Then me old eyes must be deceiving me, for methinks I saw him upon yer shoulder." Raikes regarded Peg closely.

"Indeed, you did. Does not everyone enjoy a change of scene from time to time?" Peg turned to Rosamunde and explained, "Mr. Raikes was . . . well, an old business associate of mine."

Peg then turned to the other man and said, "However, I have not the pleasure of *your* acquaintance, sir."

The hulking giant made no response.

"Gidley," Raikes answered for him. "My newest business associate."

Gidley's grimy coat was much too small for him, exposing his large hands and hairy wrists. The bright pink line of a ragged scar ran from one ear to the other across the man's throat. He merely stared silently at Rosamunde and Peg.

"Do return to the house now," Peg dismissed Rosamunde.

She walked slowly. Eavesdropping was rude, not to mention embarrassing if one were caught. Still, Rosamunde could not resist listening.

"How unexpected," she heard her uncle say. "And how very like you."

"I knew ye'd be surprised to see me."

"I had heard many years ago that you were dead," Peg said as he began to lead them down the path, away from the house.

"I'd heard the same of you, Peg. Yet, as ye can plainly see, 'twas mere ugly rumor."

They had passed beyond her range of hearing as she gained the apparent safety of the terrace.

'How strange,' she thought, frowning. 'No one would call him Peg but me.' She stopped as she suddenly realized there were others who would call him Peg. 'And his pirate friends.'

She shook her head and tried to laugh away her growing doubts. His pirate tales were all concocted to amuse her, not to mention to aggravate her stepmother. Uncle Peg had been an honest merchant seaman. He had not *really* been a pirate, had he?

Suddenly Rosamunde saw Peg's face turn ashen white.

He began to breathe in long, jagged gulps. She saw him shake his head and gesture toward the garden gate. His two unwelcome callers turned slowly and left.

"Uncle Peg, what happened?" she cried as she reached his side.

Peg shook his head. The normal color was returning to his face, but he was still breathing as if he were in great pain.

"Fine . . . I'm fine, my dear," was all he would reply. "Merely an old feud . . . best left forgotten."

—=TWO=—

Lawrence Edmonds, Viscount Merritt, could scarcely credit that he was actually here, much less that the place now belonged to him.

He stood in the hall of Penderrick Keep, frowning, until his eyes adjusted from the bright, noonday sunshine outside to the dim light which filtered in through the grimy panes of the Palladian window over the large front door.

His companion, the Honorable Roger Whitlaw, exhibited no such caution. The eerie quiet of the deserted Keep had silenced even Roger's customary volubility, but did not prevent him from roaming up and down the dusky hall, peering into a succession of darkened doorways.

As Lord Merritt's icy blue eyes grew accustomed to the dim hall, he noted the single, dust-laden pewter candelabra set upon an oaken side table, the lone piece of furniture remaining in the hall. A few worthless, time-dulled paintings hung upon the sooty paneling.

His solicitor had warned him of the poor condition in which he would find Penderrick Keep, but Mr. Newby's cursory description could not begin to encompass the true horror of the situation.

Furniture and fittings were not the only things missing, his lordship observed with increasing irritation. Where in blazes was the butler, or a footman, or even a housemaid, to greet him and his companion? He hadn't journeyed all the way from London just to be ignored by his own staff!

Lord Merritt tugged each long finger from his perfectly

fitted riding gloves. Folding the gloves neatly together, he impatiently slapped the buff leather against the palm of his hand.

He removed his tall beaver hat and placed the gloves inside. He began to set them upon the side table, but when he noticed the thick coating of dust, he quickly changed his mind.

He withdrew a silk handkerchief from his pocket and disdainfully swept away the dust. Then and only then did he place his hat upon the table. He shook out his handkerchief thoroughly, refolded it precisely along the same crease lines, and replaced it in his pocket neatly so that it did not mar the perfect lines of his jacket.

Smoothing the waves of his sandy-colored hair back into their customary order, Lord Merritt looked about him. 'Where the deuce has Roger taken himself off to now?' he wondered. ''Tis bad enough that things have been disappearing from here for years. I have no intention of allowing what *I* bring here to do likewise.'

He suppressed his impulse to call out for his missing friend. From his earliest years, his father had literally beaten into him his belief that the viscounts Merritt never actively sought out social inferiors.

'Still and all,' he decided, 'Roger has the damnedest knack for finding trouble in places where one would least expect it.'

Ostensibly to inspect his recent acquisition, Lord Merritt began to prowl about. The click of his shiny Hessians against the marred parquetry echoed through the empty hall as he peered into one room after the other. At last, he heard Roger's cheery greeting.

"Merritt! Where have you been? I feared you had been kidnapped by the resident ghost of this mausoleum."

"And I had begun to wonder what misadventure you had got into this time," his lordship scolded in an effort not to show his relief.

"As if some mishap should ever befall me!" Roger denied.

Lord Merritt strode across the bare hardwood floor to stand before one of the tall windows, covered with tightly drawn draperies. "Ever since we were boys together at Eton, you have kept me busy saving your neck from one scrape or the other."

His friend merely grinned and shrugged his shoulders.

"Roger, sometimes I wonder why I continue to associate with you."

"Because I am the closest you will ever come to laughter and excitement in your entire misbegotten life, you sore-headed old bear!" Roger declared with a hearty laugh. "The baptismal record may put you at a mere nine and twenty, yet there are times when you comport yourself as if you were just as old as King George himself."

"And there are times when you comport yourself as if you were just as mad," Lord Merritt countered. He did his best to hide his jest behind his customary mask of censure.

"I prefer to think of myself as full of *joie de vivre*," Roger replied, apparently quite used to his lordship's lack of a display of humor. "But not you, Merritt. No. Your life is encompassed by White's, and Merritt House in Cavendish Square, and Edmondston Park in Kent." With his finger, he swirled a little triangle in front of him, the better to emphasize the narrow limits of Lord Merritt's existence.

"I am quite content just as I am," Lord Merritt maintained.

"But now you have added a new dimension." Roger began to swirl a little square in front of him. "Penderrick Keep."

"I still cannot credit that when my uncle passed away, he left this dilapidated pile of wood and masonry to me," Lord Merritt said, shaking his head to indicate his disbelief.

Roger nodded, looking about. "The beauty of it is overwhelming."

Lord Merritt raised one sandy-colored brow as his only response.

"Yes, yes. I know you, Merritt." Roger waved his hand through the dust motes gliding on streams of light in the still air. "You are rarely overwhelmed."

"I find the entire situation ludicrous."

"Ludicrous that the impoverished Sir Harold Penderrick should bequeath what few worldly possessions he retained to the son of his only sister, his sole surviving kin?" Roger asked.

Lord Merritt could not bring himself to voice his answer. 'Ludicrous that I should find myself in possession of the one place in the world from which my father, while he was alive, did his best to keep me.'

His lordship reached up. With a strength which came from his own long-suppressed anger, he wrenched the moldering draperies aside. Instead of merely opening, the entire dry-rotted panel rent from its hangings. A cloud of dust billowed from the aged fabric as it tumbled to the floor.

"Ye gads, Merritt! Must you do that?" Roger exclaimed. He backed up quickly, coughing and waving his hand before his face. "This place is ghastly enough. I fully expected to see a nest of bats come flittering out of there."

Lord Merritt brushed the dust and mildew from his hands.

"What a dilemma that should pose you," Roger continued with a chuckle. "Does one inventory bats as chattels or as household ornamentation?"

"I shall leave that decision in the capable hands of my steward," his lordship replied, still unsmiling.

"I have it now," Roger declared, snapping his fingers. "They are chattels when they are on the wing. They are household ornamentation when hanging from the curtain rods."

"A veritable Solomon," Lord Merritt replied dryly. "I bow to your dazzling intellect."

"Bats on the curtain rods," Roger mused. "Just imagine,

Merritt. You may be starting an entirely new fashion. Perhaps it will become such a rage that gentlemen will take to wearing bats as fobs. Any lady who wished to consider herself the first stare of fashion would wear two as earbobs. Plump old dowagers will attach a bat or two to their turbans."

Lord Merritt sighed and shook his head. He truly believed that Roger had the jump on fashion as he already had gone quite batty.

Now that the meager contents of the room had been exposed to the glaring light of day, Roger began to roam about again. "Tell me, Merritt, is it actually as horrid as you had at first supposed?"

"No," Lord Merritt replied as he surveyed the large room. "'Tis much, much worse."

"But just look at this workmanship!" Roger exclaimed as he headed toward the huge fireplace at the other end of the room. "I don't care a fig what the place looks like now. 'Tis quite obvious that the Penderricks were once a wealthy lot."

Lord Merritt nodded. "My great-grandfather made a fortune in Carolina indigo."

Roger ran his hand over the intricate carvings of the marble mantelpiece. "Then spent it just as rapidly?"

His lordship shook his head.

"Lost upon the green baize, then?"

"No. His son, my grandfather, lost it all on a different kind of gamble, something even more unpredictable than the turn of a card."

"Aha! Then it was on the turn of a pretty ankle?" Roger suggested with a sly grin.

"Even worse. Human nature. Certain well-informed associates tried to warn my grandfather that the colonials would not be content to remain colonials forever. But I hear he was a stubborn man, declaring, 'Englishmen they are and Englishmen they shall ever be!'"

Roger nodded. "He was not alone in that sentiment."

"Of course, he was extraordinarily surprised when he

was proven wrong," Lord Merritt continued. "He barely
had time to get his money and man of affairs out of the
country before the war began."

"Not such shabby luck," Roger commented.

Lord Merritt emitted his first laugh since they had left
London for Penzance over a week ago, but it was a rueful
laugh, devoid of true humor.

"The ill luck came closer to home," his lordship explained. "Just as they rounded Lamarnah Point, a sudden
storm dashed the ship upon the rocks. Badly damaged, they
still managed to creep along. Just when they were within
sight of Penzance, they and another damaged merchant
vessel collided in the storm and sank, losing all persons and
properties aboard. Wealth and plantations gone in one
devastating blow, the Penderricks never recovered."

"Ah, now that *is* deucedly bad luck," Roger agreed.

With the toe of his boot, Lord Merritt shoved the fallen
drapery closer to the wall. He turned to gaze out the window
across the ravaged garden.

He rubbed his hand over his squared jaw. Not even to
Roger, whom he considered his closest friend, would he
disclose the fact that the one Penderrick who had suffered
the most from his grandfather's loss had been the lovely
Gwenyth, the old man's daughter and Lord Merritt's
mother.

Lack of a dowry had forced her into a loveless marriage
with the cruel Lord Merritt. After she finally accomplished
her wifely duty by producing a living son and heir almost
ten years after their marriage, his lordship had relegated
Lady Merritt to Edmondston Park and returned to his
gaming and his mistresses in London. He had not even
bothered to attend the viscountess's funeral thirteen years
later.

"Ah, well," Roger intruded upon his thoughts. "With
your fortune, you will have this place bang up to the mark
in no time."

Lord Merritt's brows drew together and his eyes changed

to an even frostier blue. "I have no intention whatsoever of using even a halfpence of Merritt money on this place."

Oblivious to his friend's irritation, Roger laughed. "Don't try to tell me the Merritt fortune is insufficient to the task. I know better, old boy."

"The Merritt fortune is to be used to maintain and improve the *Merritt* estates—" his lordship began forcefully.

"And to provide for the comfort of your lordship," Roger added. "Don't you intend to be comfortable here, Merritt?"

"I intend to sell this place," Lord Merritt announced, glancing about with utter disdain, "and be rid of it as quickly as possible."

"Lord Merritt?" exclaimed a young man who had suddenly appeared at the doorway. He was tucking his raveling shirttail into the top of his brown woolen breeches. Flaps of fabric still stuck out haphazardly behind him like some odd assortment of tails.

Lord Merritt's gaze shifted from the man's rumpled hair to his shabby shoes and up again, coldly appraising each inch and finding it greatly wanting.

"We had no idea you'd be arriving, m'lord!"

"Obviously not," his lordship remarked sarcastically. "Just who are you?"

"Me? I'm Fickle, m'lord," he answered brightly.

Glancing past the young man, his lordship noticed a young woman creeping down the stairs. With fumbling fingers, she retied the strings of her blouse and brushed her skirts to further smoothness. She tucked stray wisps of hair back up under her cotton cap, then quickly disappeared below stairs.

Lord Merritt nodded toward the vanishing girl. "I should not doubt that in the least."

Fickle flushed to the roots of his dark hair, all the while retaining a fatuous grin upon his face.

"Tell me, Fickle, just what *else* do you do around here?" Lord Merritt demanded, unsmiling.

Fickle's wide grin remained. "Why, I'm the butler, m'lord."

"Indeed?" Lord Merritt's only show of surprise was a slight raising of one brow. "Are you not a bit young to be a butler?"

Fickle shrugged his shoulders. "There are some who might say so, m'lord. But all the senior footmen had already left for other situations when the old butler passed on, and Sir Harold couldn't afford to hire an experienced one, so I went direct to butler. I was doing a good job of it, too. Sir Harold told me so himself, m'lord, right up until the day he died."

"I assume, then, that Sir Harold did not die in full possession of his faculties," Lord Merritt remarked.

"Oh, no, m'lord," Fickle protested. "Sad to say, Sir Harold was forced to sell most of his faculties."

Lord Merritt drew in a deep breath and decided to ignore the peculiar remarks of his peculiar butler, for the time being.

"Well, I am now the owner of Penderrick Keep, and I intend to make certain changes . . ."

"A wise move, m'lord," Fickle agreed readily. "If I can be of any assistance to your lordship . . ."

"Have no fear, Fickle. Certain changes come to mind immediately, and your participation in at least one of them is *most* essential."

His lordship strode across the hall toward the wide staircase. "I shall inspect the master bedchamber."

A look of panic spread over Fickle's face. "Well, m'lord . . . you see, m'lord . . ." he tried to explain as he scampered up the stairs behind his lordship. "Well, it's like this. Since Sir Harold died, it's been rather . . . well, it's been rather democratic around here."

Lord Merritt stood before the closed door where Fickle had stopped, waiting for the young butler to open it. Reluctantly, the man complied.

The white paneled door swung inward to reveal the

master bedchamber, miraculously still intact. The bedcurtains of the large mahogany bed were drawn back, revealing a mass of tumbled sheets—the remaining evidence of Fickle and the housemaid's erstwhile activities.

"I assume this is the only furnished bedchamber," his lordship said coolly.

"Oh, no, m'lord," Fickle responded. "There's the servants' quarters, and several bedchambers down the corridor, although none are as fine as this."

"I shall be staying here," Lord Merritt said. "You will escort Mr. Whitlaw to the nearest suitable guest chamber."

His lordship then strode to the small white bundle lying in the center of the room and prodded it with the toe of his boot. He bent down and, with his thumb and index finger, gingerly lifted a corner of fabric. The thin cotton drawers hung loosely from his hand.

Lord Merritt pursed his lips and looked at Fickle, who began to cough uncontrollably. Roger burst out laughing.

Without the slightest trace of amusement, his lordship tossed the drawers to Fickle. "Inform the housemaid that I should be pleased if, in the future, she would confine her possessions to her quarters."

"Do you actually intend to give Fickle the sack?" Roger exclaimed.

"Should I allow him to remain?" Lord Merritt countered. "The man is completely incompetent. I do not consider myself overly demanding, but—"

"Not you, Merritt!"

"This man is far too inexperienced to perform the services which I . . . well, which any civilized person would require of their butler."

"But he shows a certain amount of rough-hewn potential, Merritt," Roger protested. "A certain enterprising spirit . . ."

"That is the other thing which bothers me about him," his lordship continued. "How can I be certain whether the

objects which went missing from Penderrick Keep went by
my uncle's order or by Fickle's unauthorized appropria-
tion?"

"Surely you don't suspect—"

"M'lord." The sound of Fickle's voice came as a
complete surprise to Lord Merritt. He had not heard him
approach.

Fickle's hair was brushed neatly back. His face looked
newly scrubbed. He had changed from his shabby home-
spun into an equally shabby Penderrick livery. At least his
shirttails no longer peeped out between the deep green
breeches and the gold-colored waistcoat.

"Two persons await your convenience," Fickle announced with great formality.

His attempt at a more polished demeanor certainly would
lead one to believe that the man was trying to amend that
first less than satisfactory impression.

"Two persons?" Lord Merritt repeated, rising from the
delicately turned, albeit dusty, Chippendale chair. "Could
you be more specific, Fickle?"

"Well, m'lord, it's for certain they're not ladies," he
explained. "Nor do I think they'd fit into the category of
gentlemen, neither."

"B'gads, Merritt!" Roger exclaimed. "I doubt that anyone could be more specific than that! Why, even on Derby
Day at Epsom Downs, I could spot these two 'persons' from
fifty yards away."

Lord Merritt was somewhat taken aback as he entered the
drawing room. The damaged drapery was gone. The other
draperies had been drawn back to admit the afternoon's
waning sunlight. The holland covers had been removed.
The few pieces of furniture were arranged about the
fireplace. There was no fire screen, but someone had taken
a large crockery pitcher, filled it with deep purple irises, and
placed it upon the hearth.

Despite Fickle's description of his callers, Lord Merritt

was even more surprised by the sight of the two men waiting for him.

Snatching his battered hat from his head, the small man executed a series of bobbing little bows as he shuffled up to Lord Merritt.

"Raikes, at yer service, m'lord. Me associate, Gidley, and meself crave a moment o' yer valuable time."

His lordship frowned. "In what regard?"

"A certain business proposition—"

"I shan't be entrusting any of my money to the likes of you. Now begone," his lordship declared sharply.

"Oh, no, m'lord!" Raikes exclaimed. " 'Twon't require any money on yer lordship's part. All we're asking is yer lordship's cooperation."

When Lord Merritt made no reply, Raikes glanced over to Roger, then quickly back to his lordship. "If we could perhaps speak private-like for a bit, m'lord?"

Lord Merritt was certainly not afraid of these two, no matter how threatening-looking that enormous Gidley fellow might appear. However, he still felt it wisest to keep some company about him, even if only to have them as a witness to whatever "business proposition" these persons might offer.

"My business dealings have always been aboveboard, and shall remain so," he informed the man.

"No, no, m'lord," Raikes said quickly. " 'Tis nothing havy-cavy regarding this business. 'Tis just that I don't think yer lordship would want the world to be knowing yer personal and private business. And believe me, m'lord, 'tis indeed personal and particular to lost Penderrick fortunes."

Under lowered lids, Lord Merritt contemplated the little man and his large companion. The pair hardly looked as if he should believe their insistent assurances that the business was legal. What could this man know of lost Penderrick fortunes that was not only common knowledge, but also very old news?

'Still,' he decided, 'what harm could come from merely listening?'

He gestured to the chairs, indicating that his callers should be seated. Roger languidly lowered himself into a chair and slouched back. Raikes and Gidley also seated themselves. Yet, unlike Roger, they remained perched on the edge of their chairs, as if ready for an immediate departure. Lord Merritt preferred to stand, feeling that posture indicated his control of this increasingly bizarre situation.

"Please elaborate upon your business plans, Mr. Raikes."

Raikes was busily looking about him. "Appears as if the loss o' the Penderrick fortune was quite devastating," he commented.

"That is common knowledge," his lordship replied.

Raikes craned his skinny neck upward, regarding the coffered ceiling festooned with cobwebs. "The place appears to have been built soundly, however," he observed. "Shouldn't be too difficult to fix it up again . . . *if* a body had the funds."

Lord Merritt made a noncommittal shrug of his broad shoulders. He had been willing to listen to the man, but he was coming to the end of his patience with these pointless ramblings.

Suddenly Raikes lost interest in the ceiling and looked directly into Lord Merritt's cold, blue eyes. "Suppose I was to tell yer lordship that I knew where the Penderrick fortune was?"

"Then I should say you were no more intelligent than anyone else," Lord Merritt responded. "Everyone knows the Penderrick fortune sank aboard the *Dauntless* many years ago, and now lies between Penzance and Mount St. Michael, several fathoms down."

Raikes' eyes narrowed as he smiled. "Everyone *thinks* they know that. But there be one man alone who knows the true location o' the Penderrick fortune."

"The *true* location?" Roger repeated, springing upright in his chair. "At last! Now this is becoming more interesting."

Lord Merritt turned a discouraging glare upon his friend. Then he turned to the perplexing Raikes. "I suppose *you* are that one man."

" 'Tis not I, m'lord," Raikes protested.

"No? Then what sum are you demanding to disclose the identity of the man who does know?"

Raikes' hard, weather-beaten face took on an expression of the utmost personal injury. "Surely not *demanding*, m'lord. 'Tis only a request from yer humble servants. A share o' the fortune once it be found."

"Sounds fair enough to me, Merritt," Roger commented. "If no fortune is found, you owe them nothing."

"Do hush, Roger," Lord Merritt ordered, completely exasperated.

His lordship frowned in deep concentration. He turned to the little man. "Are you that certain of your knowledge, then, that you would postpone payment until the fortune is found?"

"Oh, 'twill be found, m'lord," Raikes assured him. "We're that certain."

This entire situation was preposterous, Lord Merritt decided. Why should this disreputable man claim to know something more regarding the Penderrick fortune than anyone else? Why should he have waited nearly forty years to disclose this knowledge?

As Lord Merritt considered the empty mansion which was falling apart about his very ears, the image of his mother rose before his eyes. Alternately badgered, beaten, and neglected—a sad and sorry woman, made old before her time. How different her life would have been if the Penderrick fortune had not been lost!

Little good finding it would do her now. On the other hand, did he not owe it to his mother at least to make the attempt, even if the offer was coming from such an outlandish quarter?

"If you know the identity of this singular gentleman, why do you not confront him yourself?" Lord Merritt asked.

"Well, we be honest folk, m'lord," Raikes answered, glancing over to Gidley, then back to Lord Merritt. "The fortune be yers, in truth. We only wish a small portion fer our troubles."

Raikes rubbed his stubbly chin with his grimy hand. "And, ye see, m'lord, we've already spoken with the gentleman in question, and, well, he's rather uncooperative. We thought perhaps that he might be more willing to disclose the whereabouts to yer lordship. If ye could speak to him, without mentioning us, o' course . . ."

"Of course." Lord Merritt nodded with understanding. "Then tell me, who is this gentleman?"

"A Mr. Dudley Wickes at Eglantine Cottage, neighboring yer lordship's very own property," Raikes replied. "He was the cabin boy aboard the *Halverton*."

Raikes leaned forward in his chair. His eyes narrowed and his voice grew low. "Ye see, he and the captain o' the *Halverton* boarded the foundering *Dauntless* and took the fortune and whatever else they could grab before the ship went down, heedless o' what other lives were lost. They brought the chest ashore and hid it somewhere near here."

"Why should I believe your preposterous tale?" Lord Merritt demanded. He clenched his jaw, the better to subdue his own growing interest in the man's tale.

"Because, m'lord, *I* was the first mate aboard the *Halverton*."

Lord Merritt was silent for an exceptionally long time. Raikes and Gidley sat very still in the fine chairs, but Roger began to fidget.

"I shall need some time to consider your proposal, Raikes," his lordship said at length.

"Oh, come now, Merritt!" Roger exclaimed. "What is

there to contemplate? 'Tis a treasure hunt, pure and simple. Are there clues to follow? Does 'X' mark the spot?"

"Oh, *do* hush, Roger!" Lord Merritt scolded.

"Sounds like jolly good fun, if you ask me," Roger persisted. "Has it all over sitting about watching this pile of dust molder away."

"Do be thinking quick-like, m'lord," Raikes said, "as the gentleman in question be in rather delicate health, if ye take me meaning."

Lord Merritt began to walk toward the doorway, signifying that the interview was concluded.

"We'll be staying at the Dead Man's Head Inn," Raikes informed his lordship as he and Gidley rose to leave. "Ye've only to summon us, m'lord."

—THREE—

"Mr. Wickes, remove yourself from that garden immediately and greet your callers," Mrs. Wickes commanded.

Mr. Wickes looked from the extremely interesting roots of the rosebush up to his extraordinarily tedious wife.

"You managed to avoid Mr. Shelby yesterday, traipsing all over the fields instead," she scolded.

"But, Catherine, I'm a country squire," he protested. "I'm *supposed* to traipse all over the fields."

"Well, you shan't today!"

"Why? Who has come calling now?"

"Lord Merritt!" Mrs. Wickes declared triumphantly. When Mr. Wickes failed to show the appropriate appreciation for the importance of their guest, she continued, "I know for a certainty, for I heard it from the Widow Camberton, that his lordship is handsome, wealthy, and *unmarried*."

"Well then, even if his lordship has come to call upon me—although I cannot think why—it does not signify, as you will soon monopolize his time for Mary Ann."

"Can you blame a mother for trying?" she accused. "I have done my utmost to secure Mr. Shelby for Rosamunde, in spite of the ungrateful girl's complete disregard for him. But there is no one in Penzance whom I consider suitable for Mary Ann, and we most assuredly cannot afford to travel to London to find her a husband."

Mrs. Wickes clasped her hands to her bosom and cast her

28

eyes upward. "Then Heaven drops a viscount directly into our laps! An answer to a mother's prayer!"

Unimpressed, Mr. Wickes began to apply a trowel of cow manure to the base of the rosebush. Mrs. Wickes seized his elbow and hauled him to his feet. The cow manure went sprinkling across the brick walk.

"Come now. We must not leave his lordship waiting too long in that sitting room," she ordered. "He might notice how shabby the place is."

She seized the trowel from his hand and discarded it in the bushes. Time enough to retrieve it later. She detached the leather apron from about her husband's thin waist and tossed that, too.

"I can only hope that Dudley and that wretched bird have not chosen this time to make a most inappropriate appearance," she lamented.

She spun Mr. Wickes about to face her. "Oh, dear, you still smell of manure," she wailed as she straightened his wilted cravat. "Well, there's little to be done for it now."

As she dragged her husband up the walk and across the terrace, Mrs. Wickes was joyously forming a grand picture in her mind. Her very own little Mary Ann, resplendent in endless lengths of white satin, gossamer silk, and fine French lace, was being escorted by Mr. Wickes up the aisle of the private chapel at Penderrick Keep. Why, even the Prince Regent himself was in attendance . . .

"More rum, wench! Or I'll hang the lot o' ye from the yardarm!" Sir Polly's sharp demand met her ears as she reached the doorway.

Mrs. Wickes' grand wedding plans vanished in an explosion of parrot feathers.

"We have visitors," Mary Ann said as she entered the bedchamber she and Rosamunde shared. "Mama says not to dally." She stood waiting.

Rosamunde wished she could obtain more information

from her quiet stepsister. She descended the narrow stair-case, followed by Mary Ann.

'She could not even have come downstairs if she had not *followed* me,' Rosamunde thought, feeling ever more disgusted with the timid girl.

"The good ship *Dorcas May* be four days out o' Kingston when the gale broke upon us," Peg's rasping voice carried out into the hall. "The navigator be roaring drunk and washed overboard at the first blow."

Rosamunde smiled as she heard her uncle retelling one of his best tales.

"So there we be, in the midst o' the Sargasso, with every star in God's creation spread overhead and nary a soul aboard who knew how to read their secrets."

The callers were new, Rosamunde deduced. No one but she and Mary Ann ever listened to Uncle Peg's tales—Rosamunde because she never tired of them, and Mary Ann because she had not the courage to excuse herself when he began.

"Becalmed for a fortnight we were." Peg sat in his fireside chair. Sir Polly stalked back and forth and pivoted upon his shoulder. "The rum ran out. The water turned a foul and blackish brew. The bosun's mate ran mad and threw himself to Davy Jones."

Peg raised his gnarled hand to his brow and stared into some unseen distance. "Then we saw her, her sails as white and billowing as the mist through which she came."

Two well-dressed strangers were seated upon the blue damask sofa. One gentleman was dark-haired and lounged quite at ease upon the worn and lumpy cushions, grinning broadly as he listened.

"A grappling hook were tossed aboard and a keg o' fresh water, sweet as honey to a parched man's lips, were swung across, then the lines were loosed. She flew no flag nor insignia, but that be no reason to refuse her welcomed gift."

Rosamunde's eyes were drawn to the gentleman who sat closest to her uncle. He held himself erect, as if his spine were the rigid mast of the ship which Peg still dreamed he sailed. The man's hair was the palest brown, almost blond. He listened, attentive as his companion. Yet, unlike his companion, he showed no sign of amused disbelief at Peg's outlandish yarn. He appeared so aloof, so cold and forbidding. Why then were her eyes strangely riveted to him?

"We followed her—what choice had we? For three days and nights, the captain never slept, never left the wheel, never took his eye from that ship. Yet, nary a soul hailed us from the bridge, nor did we ever, man or boy of us, see a single face at a porthole."

Peg's voice dropped to barely above a whisper. "On the fourth day, I mounted to the crow's nest, and on the horizon, I spotted Kingston Harbor. All eyes turned to our destination. When we turned back to the phantom ship that was our salvation, she be gone—vanished into the mist from whence she came."

"Lord Merritt, what a great honor you do our humble home!" Mrs. Wickes' syrupy voice provided an abrupt, unwelcomed end to Peg's ghostly tale.

Rosamunde frowned with disappointment. Stepmama had not even allowed one the time for a delicious shiver following the conclusion of the story.

"Avast, lads, there she blows!" Sir Polly cried.

The dark-haired man chuckled.

Mrs. Wickes, with Mr. Wickes following silently behind, sailed boldly toward the fair-haired gentleman. Rosamunde took this opportunity to advance into the room. Mary Ann followed, close as a shadow, upon her heels.

Lord Merritt rose and bowed ever so slightly.

"And your companion . . . ?" Mrs. Wickes inquired, blatantly appraising his worthiness as a match for Mary Ann.

"Mr. Roger Whitlaw," that gentleman replied, bowing. All the while, the cheerful smile never left his face.

"Mister?"

"Just like a piece of great literature still in the works,"

Mr. Whitlaw replied with a grin, "I am—alas!—untitled."

Rosamunde thought that Stepmama managed to hide her disappointment rather well.

"My lord, may I present my daughter, Miss Mary Ann Bellows?" Completely bypassing Rosamunde, Mrs. Wickes reached out to grasp Mary Ann by the wrist and pull her to stand in front of Lord Merritt.

Of course, the girl was too timid to bid his lordship and his friend good day, or even to raise her eyes to theirs, Rosamunde thought. She watched with disgust as her stepsister merely dropped a shy and silent curtsey.

"How delightful to make your acquaintance, Miss Bellows," Mr. Whitlaw said. Rosamunde watched him take in Mary Ann's fragile beauty with an approving smile.

Mary Ann had that effect on most men, Rosamunde noted. She also noted that Lord Merritt's reaction had been a mere polite nod.

'Why, the man grows colder by the moment,' she marveled.

"Is this your other daughter?" Mr. Whitlaw asked as he also turned that pleasant smile upon Rosamunde.

"Oh, this is only my stepdaughter, Rosamunde."

Lord Merritt also turned to her. Rosamunde tried to smile politely at him as well, but all she could manage to do was swallow hard.

His lordship's eyes were so hard and silver-blue that she supposed they might be mirrors in which she could view her own reflection, if she dared to venture close enough. His lordship seemed to carry his own air of forbidding chill about him, which made her doubt that he would allow anyone that near.

Yet Rosamunde dared to meet his gaze. Once, briefly, his icy eyes swept up and down her figure. The look he gave her held more than mere approval, causing an unaccountable warmth to rise inside her.

"I am sorry if we have kept your lordship waiting," Mrs. Wickes apologized.

"Listening to such a stirring tale, we barely noticed the time," Mr. Whitlaw interposed.

"Oh, you truly should not pay any mind whatsoever to my poor brother-in-law's ramblings," Mrs. Wickes protested. "He's rather . . . you know . . ." She tapped her temple with her forefinger.

"Really?" Mr. Whitlaw remarked with surprise. "I found Mr. Wickes to be quite lucid. How strange that you should think him—" he tapped his own temple—"you know . . ."

Rosamunde smiled. She liked Mr. Whitlaw more and more. But as for Lord Merritt, my gracious! The man was even more reticent than the Silent Vicar, if that were possible. At least Mr. Shelby exuded a certain warmth which made his silence almost endearing. Lord Merritt, on the other hand, was approximately as warm as the waters of Penzance Harbor in mid-January. She had yet to see him smile.

"Would you care to view our garden, my lord, while our housemaid prepares some refreshments?" Mrs. Wickes suggested to Lord Merritt.

Rosamunde blinked and stared. Had Stepmama gone as mad as she purported Uncle Peg to be? They had no housemaid! Oh, there was Molly, from the village, who came every other day but Sunday to help tidy up, but she hardly counted.

"The garden is my husband's particular interest," Mrs. Wickes continued, glaring at Mr. Wickes as if trying to propel him into action by the mere force of her will.

At last, Mr. Wickes said, "If it would please your lordship and Mr. Whitlaw to follow me . . ."

Without a word, Lord Merritt extended his arm to Mrs. Wickes.

"Oh, my lord, I must supervise the housemaid—she's new, you know," she demurred, while maneuvering Mary Ann to his lordship's side. "However, Mary Ann will be pleased to accompany you."

Rosamunde could have throttled her stepmother. How could the woman be so lacking in subtlety?

Lord Merritt turned to Peg, who was still seated in his chair. "Mr. Wickes, would you care to come stroll with us? I should enjoy hearing another of your exciting yarns," he suggested.

Rosamunde turned to Lord Merritt. She had begun to believe his lordship was so wealthy that he had hired Mr. Whitlaw to speak for him. Apparently his lordship *could* speak, and without the aid of Mr. Whitlaw, either.

"I think you may find a walk more interesting than watching the housemaid," his lordship continued.

"Ye think rightly, m'lord," Peg answered as he slowly raised his gaunt form from the chair. "Especially if you've seen what manner o' creature dares call itself our housemaid!"

Mr. Whitlaw smiled and extended his arm to Rosamunde. She offered him a polite smile instead.

"You will understand if I find it more necessary to assist my uncle, won't you?" she whispered quite confidentially to him.

Mr. Whitlaw glanced at Peg's wooden leg and nodded.

Mr. Wickes was already out the doors and heading across the terrace. The one great love of his life was his garden, a subject upon which he could expound ad nauseam. Mr. Whitlaw stepped lively in order to catch up to him.

Although Peg had offered Rosamunde his arm, it was she who supported him as they strolled along. She watched Mary Ann and the equally silent Lord Merritt as they preceded them down the winding garden path.

Peg nodded at the pair. "They look rather well together, don't they?"

Rosamunde had to admit, small and slender Mary Ann, her fair curls flowing behind her, did look the perfect complement to the tall, broad-shouldered figure of his lordship.

But Mary Ann merely strolled silently beside him, and

his lordship strode along looking straight ahead all the while.

"Stepmama has quite a vivid imagination when it comes to matchmaking for Mary Ann. How can she envisage two such reticent people together?" she whispered to Uncle Peg. "At least when Mary Ann walks with Mr. Shelby, they manage to find *some* conversation between them, even if it is only the condition of the heathen in India."

Peg smiled at her and raised one bushy eyebrow mischievously. "Conversation is not everything."

Rosamunde felt oddly reluctant to acknowledge any suitability between her silent stepsister and the glacial Lord Merritt. "Fancy his lordship being interested in your old sea tales," she said, changing the subject.

"Why not?" Peg defended himself. "I spin a damned good yarn, lass."

Suddenly Peg clutched his left arm tightly to his side as if in great pain. He stumbled and would have fallen to the rough bricks were it not for Rosamunde.

"Uncle Peg!" she cried as she tried to brace him.

He was a gaunt, old man, yet heavy in his helplessness. Rosamunde felt her own knees begin to buckle under his weight.

Lord Merritt's arm stretched across Peg's bony chest and lifted the elderly man upright.

"I have you, old fellow," Lord Merritt reassured him. His words were hearty, but his voice soothing.

Rosamunde still supported Peg on one side, while his lordship slid his arm about the old man's back and held him upright. She was close enough to Lord Merritt now that she could actually look into his eyes. Over the top of the old man's wizened head, Rosamunde saw her own deep concern for Uncle Peg mirrored in his lordship's silver-blue eyes.

"Thank you, my lord," Rosamunde whispered, breathless with exertion.

"Are you quite all right yourself, Miss Wickes?" Lord Merritt asked.

She could accept that his lordship might be concerned for one who was truly ill, but the concern for her so apparent in his low voice was quite unexpected.

"Oh, I'm fine, my lord," she replied automatically, unsure of any other response she might make to this enigmatic man.

"Back to the house," Peg murmured in a hoarse whisper. "Quickly, my girl."

"Shall I lift you, old fellow?" Lord Merritt asked.

"Not at all, my lord," he protested, then gave a weak laugh. "I've always carried my own weight."

"Quite so," his lordship agreed. He felt strangely abashed—quite an unusual sensation for him—that he might have embarrassed the elderly man in his affliction.

He and Rosamunde assisted Peg up the steps and across the terrace.

"Uncle Peg's room is in that direction," Rosamunde told him, indicating their destination with a nod of her dark head.

"Belay that bilge!" Peg fussed.

"Belay that bilge!" Sir Polly echoed.

"I'll sit in my chair," Peg said.

"But you're ill, Uncle Peg—" Rosamunde protested.

"My chair!" he insisted.

Peg turned to Lord Merritt and winked slyly. "The only time a pirate should accept dying in bed is when he has luscious company there."

Much to his surprise, Lord Merritt almost found himself chuckling with genuine amusement. Quickly, he resumed his habitual impassive countenance. From the corner of his eye, he glanced over to Miss Wickes. What would her reaction be to Dudley Wickes' innuendos?

Most of the young misses of his acquaintance would simper and blush at such suggestive remarks. Then again, there were some ladies—if one could style them thus—who would not only laugh at the old pirate's jest, but could best any lewd remark he made.

Miss Wickes was smiling! Well, he had certainly not expected that type of reaction from a sheltered, country-bred miss.

He watched her more closely. Her fine, rosy lips were parted in a smile of mere indulgent humor rather than outright amusement.

"Well then, Uncle Peg," she said, "since there appears to be no luscious company currently available, let us get you into your chair."

"Right, my girl," Peg agreed. "But let's keep that bed in readiness just in case some luscious company does make an unexpected appearance."

His lordship assisted Rosamunde to settle the old man into his chair by the fire. She slid a footstool closer so he could prop up his leg.

"More rum, wench!" Sir Polly demanded. He lifted one foot and set it down, turning about on the back of Uncle Peg's chair. Then he lifted the other foot and turned in the opposite direction. "Heave to, ye pox-ridden doxy! More rum!"

"Capital idea, Polly," Peg agreed.

"Do you think you should, Uncle Peg?" Rosamunde asked.

"If a pirate cannot die with a beautiful woman in his arms, the least he could have is a jug o' rum in his hands."

"I'll see if I can find a *mug*," she promised him, heading for the door to the hallway.

Lord Merritt could not resist following her across the narrow hall to the room opposite, which apparently was Mr. Wickes' study.

"Are you in need of assistance, Miss Wickes?" he asked from the doorway.

She looked at him with her gray-blue eyes and smiled. It was not the same indulgent smile she had used for her sick, old uncle. Nor was it the polite smile he had seen her

bestow upon Roger. It certainly was not one of the
flirtatious smiles so many London misses directed at him. It
was one of gratitude, certainly, he decided, for his care of
her ailing uncle. There was also something else—yet
unidentified—there.

She opened a chinoiserie cabinet.

"Thank you, my lord, but the mug is much lighter than
Uncle Peg," she answered, indicating a small stoppered
brown jug. She grinned at him. "I think I can manage."

"Of course, Miss Wickes," his lordship replied. He
watched her uncork the jug, then pour out just a small
amount of the brown liquid into the mug.

Her dark hair curled softly about her ivory cheeks. Her
slender fingers curved gently about the mug as she filled it.
Lord Merritt was seized with an impulse to take her hands
into his own, to smooth his hand down her soft cheek.

'Don't be absurd, Merritt!' he chided himself. He was
here for information, not amusement. Making an attempt at
a more detached point of view, Lord Merritt assessed
Rosamunde.

Her hair was neatly arranged. Her pale green round gown
was plain, and certainly not in the latest fashion, but
immaculate nonetheless. She was undoubtedly closer to her
uncle than anyone else in her family. She appeared to be a
sensible young woman, Lord Merritt decided, stroking his
chin. Perhaps she would be a reliable source of information
regarding what her uncle might know of the lost fortune.

"Pray, excuse me, my lord," she said, stepping around
him in order to return to her uncle.

Lord Merritt was surprised to find that he had instinctively moved closer to her as he had been watching her.

"A moment, please." He laid his hand briefly on her arm
to detain her. She startled, as if he had touched her with ice.
Reluctantly, he withdrew his hand. "Your uncle tells a
rousing story."

"He enjoys recounting his old sea tales," she answered

with her usual indulgent smile. "And I never tire of hearing them."

"If he feels equal to the task, I, too, should like to hear more," Lord Merritt suggested.

Her cool gray-blue eyes met his. "Perhaps at a later time, my lord, in view of his present condition."

"Indeed, indeed," Lord Merritt agreed readily. He paused, then continued. "Then he does have more tales to tell?"

"My uncle has an imagination as vast as the seas he once sailed," she answered.

"But are his tales true?" his lordship asked.

She laughed, a light little sound that fluttered through his hearing. She eyed him mockingly.

"Surely, my lord, *you* don't believe in ghostly ships!"

Lord Merritt felt his hackles rise. How dare this country miss mock him! Still, he found himself smiling as the absurdity of his own question dawned upon him.

He overpowered the smile before it ever gave him away by reaching his lips. "No, Miss Wickes. Indeed not."

—FOUR—

"Quite an unusual visit, Merritt," Roger commented as they rode back toward Penderrick Keep in the gathering twilight.

"Indeed," Lord Merritt replied with a single nod.

As they had ridden toward Eglantine Cottage, Lord Merritt was uncertain as to what he might encounter from a purported former pirate and his family. Now, having been there, he was still uncertain of what he had found.

An overbearing lady, certainly, and her henpecked husband and painfully shy daughter. An ailing old man who claimed to have been a pirate but who most probably was merely out of his mind. The old man's extremely unusual pet. And the niece—ah yes, what of Miss Rosamunde Wickes? Lord Merritt mused.

"I vow!" Roger's jovial complaint intruded into Lord Merritt's contemplation. "If I had to listen to Mr. Wickes expound upon rosebushes, rainfall, and manure for one more minute, I would run mad from the garden."

"A little education in agricultural science would not harm you," Lord Merritt told his friend.

"How did you broaden *your* education while you were there, Merritt?" Roger asked, a teasing smile spread across his face.

Lord Merritt merely shrugged. After he departed Eton, he determined never again to bear standing examination—and certainly not from Roger.

When he received no response, Roger said, "I doubt that Mrs. Wickes knows anything of the treasure."

Lord Merritt gave a short, derisive laugh. "If she did, the entire county would know of it by now."

Roger nodded his hearty agreement. "But I'll wager you will hear nothing of pirates, phantom ships, and lost treasure from Miss Bellows."

"Indeed." With a small lift of his eyebrow, Lord Merritt agreed. "Rarely have I encountered a young lady of a more retiring demeanor."

"After you left with Miss Wickes, *I* was left to escort her about the garden. 'Tis a wonder I did not fall asleep in my tracks."

"My sympathies, Roger," Lord Merritt said. "I do appreciate how you suffer for me."

"Old Peg was certainly entertaining, though," Roger said more brightly.

"The man has an extraordinary imagination," Lord Merritt agreed. "Unfortunately, I do not think he knows anything of treasure, either."

"Do you think Miss Wickes does?" Roger asked.

Lord Merritt shook his head. "I could not say."

"She appears to be quite close to her uncle." Roger cast Lord Merritt a sly look. "And you appeared to be interested in questioning *her* further."

Lord Merritt looked scornfully at Roger. "If you believe that, your imagination is even more extraordinary than Dudley Wickes'."

"I did not imagine your quickness to offer her your assistance when Peg fell."

"Anyone else would have done the same," Lord Merritt said, depreciating his magnanimous gesture.

"Nor did Miss Wickes seem the least bit reluctant to accept your help," Roger added with a suggestive wink.

"She *needed* my assistance," Lord Merritt insisted. "The old man is deceptively heavy."

"Indeed he must have been," Roger answered, "to require your assistance *all that time* . . ."

"Well, if the old fellow was about to die, I had to be there," Lord Merrit answered gruffly. "Suppose he should decide to disclose, with his last gasping breath, the location of my family's fortune, and I should miss it all?"

"I think you would prefer not to miss his niece, either."

Lord Merritt opened his mouth to give another excuse, but none would come. He frowned. He really ought to think up something, or Roger, with nothing else to occupy his mind in this remote corner of the country, would tease him unmercifully the remainder of the evening. The trouble was, Roger was right. Lord Merritt owned, to himself alone, that he would indeed enjoy seeing Miss Wickes, just once more.

"Best not pay Miss Wickes more attention than you pay Miss Bellows," Roger warned, "lest you incur the wrath of the formidable Mrs. Wickes."

"I have no intention of paying attention to either young lady," Lord Merritt snapped. "I went there in search of information, and for nothing else."

"Well, sometimes one encounters things which one was not expecting," Roger reminded him. "The ladies *are* rather lovely."

Lord Merritt shook his head.

"I'm certain Miss Bellows' mother is looking to make a brilliant match for her," Roger observed. "Perhaps even a viscount."

"Doubtless she will try," Lord Merritt answered with a humorless chuckle. "But I think, over the years, I have gained enough experience in avoiding matchmaking mamas to circumvent even the ambitious Mrs. Wickes."

"Miss Wickes is a bit older than her stepsister and appears to be heading for the shelf," Roger continued. Carefully, he studied his lordship. "She might not mind a small dalliance . . ."

"I think not!" Lord Merritt declared sharply.

"Well, she's not *that* horrid, Merritt."

"Miss Wickes may be virtually penniless and a bit past her prime, but she is still an honorable lady," Lord Merritt asserted. "You know perfectly well I have never been in the line of seduction. I never thought you were either—"

Roger began to laugh.

Lord Merritt regarded him cautiously. Indeed, the man *had* heard too much from Mr. Wickes about rosebushes, rainfall, and manure, and *had* run mad. It had just taken a little while for Mr. Wickes' dissertation to take effect.

"Do you know what I think, Merritt?" Roger asked, still laughing. "I think you are being highly defensive regarding the reputation of a lady whose acquaintance you have just made."

Lord Merritt raised one dark brow to a haughty angle. "An honorable man is always concerned for the honor of a young lady gently bred. *I* have always been an honorable man."

"Indeed, you are. For as long as I have known you, you have also been a man who has precious little sense of humor. For pity's sake, Merritt, for as long as you have known *me*, you should surely be able to tell when I am jesting." Roger gave an injured sniff. "I thought myself rather clever, too."

Well, perhaps he had been just a bit too harsh with his friend, Lord Merritt decided. He knew that Roger aspired to be a wit, even though he did not always succeed.

His lordship grimaced. Heretofore, he had regarded Roger's feeble jests with amused detachment. He had rarely taken offense at any of them. What in heaven's name had affected him that he should be quite so defensive now?

Oh, Miss Wickes was pretty enough with her pale skin, shining chestnut hair, and soft, gray-blue eyes, but then again, so were many of the young ladies he had encountered. If the truth be told, there were those who even surpassed her.

She was certainly kind and solicitous for her aging old pirate of an uncle, but then, many women could be kind.

She appeared to be intelligent when conversing. Well, in that, he conceded, she did indeed surpass many of the ladies of his acquaintance.

He was merely overwrought by the lengthy journey he had just made in Roger's garrulous company. The abysmal condition of Penderrick Keep and the strangely proposed recovery of the lost fortune delivered by an equally strange pair of men had not helped his disposition. A hearty dinner and a sound night's sleep, Lord Merritt decided, were what he needed to put him to rights.

Still, Lord Merritt could not help but shake his head in dismay when Penderrick Keep came into view.

His horse stumbled up the rutted gravel drive. The large expanse of lawn was overgrown into a tangled wilderness. Indeed, the exterior of Penderrick Keep was as unkept as the interior. Neither a decent meal nor a decent rest would be got in this dismal place.

The large front door swung open immediately as he had put his foot upon the first step. His lordship paused, supposing Roger's imaginary resident ghost was up to some trick.

'Twas only Fickle, his lordship noted with just a bit of relief, and not an inconsiderable amount of surprise. The man actually *did* work at Penderrick Keep.

Lord Merritt paused with surprise when he entered the hall. The light of the setting sun streamed in through the sparkling clean panes of the large Palladian window above the door. The paneling had been scrubbed. The lone table in the hall had been polished. There was little remedy for the marred floor, but it, too, was swept and scrubbed clean.

Lord Merritt ran his index finger over the frame of one of the paintings hanging upon the wall. He rubbed his thumb and forefinger together. Not a spot of dust remained.

"Merritt!" Roger exclaimed. "We're in the wrong house!"

Lord Merritt proceeded down the hall and opened a door. The only ornamentation in the dark room was the moth-eaten red velvet draperies, festooned with gold cording and cobwebs.

"No, Roger. This is the correct house, more's the pity," his lordship said. With a deep sigh, he closed the door. He looked about the clean hall again. "Still, 'tis quite a miraculous transformation, I must own."

"Your dinner is this way, m'lord," Fickle said, gesturing toward the drawing room.

Lord Merritt and Roger were seated on two mismatched chairs arranged at either end of a card table which had been set up before the fireplace.

" 'Tis Grace, the housemaid's, doing, m'lord," Fickle said as he served them.

Roger grinned. "How gratifying to know that she, too, does other things here."

"Of course, m'lord, it would be so much easier for her if she had a bit more help," Fickle suggested.

"What do you consider a bit more help?" Lord Merritt asked, casting an inquiring glance at his butler.

"Might I suggest my aunt, m'lord," Fickle answered readily. "She's a widow of good character—"

"Very well, Fickle," Lord Merritt agreed.

"Makes no use of tobacco nor strong spirits—"

"Very well, Fickle," his lordship repeated.

"Wouldn't eat much—"

"Very well," Lord Merritt said more forcefully. "You may send for her."

Why on earth had he agreed? Lord Merritt asked himself. And so quickly? Of course, he had been happy to see the small improvements that had already been made to Pender-rick Keep. But he did not intend to stay here. It should not matter to him if the place eventually fell into complete ruin.

"I thought you had no intention of staffing this place, Merritt," Roger reminded him. "That you were going to sell it immediately."

"I did. I shall," his lordship insisted. "I . . . I simply see no harm in allowing a poor widow to earn a few extra shillings by honest work. And perhaps it would not be such a bad idea to tidy up the place before I sell it."

Indeed, not a bad idea at all, his lordship decided. No doubt a better appearance would bring a better price. And doing so under the guise of charity appeared to satisfy Roger.

However, in spite of the housemaid's efforts, from time to time while Lord Merritt and Roger ate, large flakes of white paint from the plaster ceiling drifted down upon them. Lord Merritt regarded them, pondering whether these flakes might be more tasty than the meal set before them.

"What *are* these things, Merritt?" Roger asked. He pushed the small chunks he had found in the sauce toward the pile of half-green, half-black burnt peas. "I assume they are safe to eat, although I myself have postponed consuming them until I can be assured of their identity."

"You should have asked me sooner, Roger," Lord Merritt replied, tactfully ignoring similar chunks on his own plate. "Although I doubt you will believe me, they are pieces of apple."

"Apple?"

"Apple."

"In the meat sauce?" Roger said with disbelief. He poked at the small chunks. "Pray tell, Merritt, is it an old Penderrick family receipt, long kept secret?"

He speared a chunk with his fork and placed it in his mouth. As he chewed, an expression of disgust spread over his face. "I can easily see why 'twas kept secret."

"I merely identified the pieces for you, Roger. I never said you had to eat them."

Fickle cleared the empty plates, then served each gentleman a large slice of an undetermined type of pie.

Roger cautiously lifted the soggy crust and peeked under it. "Well, apparently the cook did not use up all the apples in the meat sauce."

Not wishing to appear too apprehensive, Lord Merritt examined his own slice with a bit more discretion. He frowned.

"There is more to this pie than apples," his lordship said. He rolled a small, white sphere from the filling. "What are these things?"

Roger excavated his filling until he found an identical sphere. He speared it and held it up for examination. "Grapes? Gooseberries?" he offered, sniffing the white globule.

"Pickled onions," Fickle answered.

Lord Merritt merely raised one eyebrow in surprise.

Roger's fork clattered noisily to his plate. "I say, old man, you *are* carrying this secret family receipt thing a bit too far, don't you think?"

"Now you see how far Penderrick Keep has fallen, m'lord," Fickle said. He hung his head in what Lord Merritt could only assume was his butler's impression of abject resignation. "*You* need only suffer through these meals for the duration of your stay, m'lord. *We*'ve been having to eat this swill for *months*!"

"My condolences," Lord Merritt said. "How did Penderrick Keep arrive at this culinary catastrophe?"

Fickle drew in a deep breath of relief. "Ah, 'tis one small thing for which we can be thankful, that Cook has not taken to stewing cats."

"Fickle," Lord Merritt said, deciding to try again for some sensible explanation from his butler, "what happened to the cook?"

"Well, he's rather old, m'lord," Fickle said. "From what I've heard, he's been in service here since Sir Harold, may he rest in peace, was but a lad. And he tends to become a bit confused," Fickle said. "Sir Harold was intending to pension him off and hire another, but . . ." He shrugged his shoulders.

"There is little point in acquiring a new cook for the few weeks I shall be staying here," Lord Merritt reasoned.

"Merritt!" Roger exclaimed. He poked at the mixture of onions and apples on his plate. "What have I ever done to you to deserve a punishment such as this?"

"It hardly warrants sending all the way to London for my chef . . ."

"By the time he could arrive, I shall be dead of starvation—or food poisoning!" Roger wailed.

"If I may be so bold, m'lord," Fickle interjected. "My mother raised a large family, and none of us starved." He bowed to Roger. "Nor died—at least not of food poisoning. I'm certain my mum could be hired—for a reasonable sum, m'lord. Mind you, 'twould be plain fare, but excellent."

"I'm willing to chance it, Merritt," Roger said eagerly.

"Well, I suppose it would do no harm to have edible meals while we are here. Send for her," Lord Merritt agreed, waving his butler away.

But Fickle remained standing at his lordship's side. "Mum is very good with vegetables, m'lord."

"If she can discern apples from onions, I shall be pleased," Roger said.

"And my father is quite a good gardener," he continued. "Why, he could coax that little patch of soil behind the kitchens into producing all sorts of delights for your lordship's enjoyment."

Lord Merritt was tired—and still hungry. He was in no state to discuss Fickle's family's varied talents. He impatiently tapped his forefinger on the table in front of him.

"I suppose your father could be persuaded to come work here, too—for a reasonable sum."

"Yes, m'lord. And with the rest of the gardens brought up to scratch, why, I'll wager you could sell this property in no time at all."

Lord Merritt suppressed a renegade grin which he felt rising to his lips. He was a cautious man, but not inordinately suspicious. Why did he have the distinct feeling that Fickle had orchestrated this entire after-dinner conversation?

"Very well, Fickle," Lord Merritt said, holding up his hands in resignation. "You may send for your father as well."

"Capital idea, Merritt," Roger said enthusiastically. "Tell me, Fickle, do you think your mother can be here to prepare breakfast tomorrow?"

Before Fickle could respond, Lord Merritt rose and said, "I expect to have a decent breakfast tomorrow morning when I return from inspecting the estate."

Roger groaned. "I hope you do not expect me to accompany you, Merritt. You know I do not adapt readily to country hours."

"Somehow I shall manage without you," Lord Merritt conceded. "However, the next day I should wish your company in the afternoon as I intend to pay another visit to Eglantine Cottage." Quite deliberately, he added, "To talk to Dudley Wickes, if he is equal to a visit."

Lord Merritt turned to Fickle. "Have my horse ready tomorrow at six."

"Ah, regarding your fine horses, m'lord . . ."

Lord Merritt frowned with apprehension. He still harbored his suspicions regarding the means by which the contents of Penderrick Keep had gone missing. Could his butler be trusted not to sell off the horseflesh while his lordship slept?

"Now, they are fine horses, m'lord," Fickle said. "And though it's been a rare treat caring for the likes of them, they deserve better than I can give."

Lord Merritt suppressed another chuckle. "I have the strangest presentiment that you are about to suggest someone who can give them such care—for a reasonable sum. Perhaps even someone who is closely related to you."

"My cousin, m'lord, has the uncanniest knack with horses." Fickle leaned a bit closer to his lordship and whispered, " 'Tis said by some of the less charitable members of the family that his mother was consorting with gypsies some nine months before his birth, if you take my meaning . . ."

Lord Merritt pursed his lips and nodded his comprehension. He had no cause to worry that Fickle would steal his horses. He'd let his cousin take care of the matter!

"I suppose this cousin could come for a reasonable sum?" Lord Merritt asked, although he knew the answer full well.

"Well, m'lord, the man has a wife . . . and children . . ."

"How many?"

"Oh, only one wife, m'lord."

"How many *children*?"

Fickle grimaced. "Seven, m'lord."

Children in his household? Lord Merritt had rarely considered the possibility, and on those infrequent occasions when he did, it was with a certain amount of distaste. Now they were to descend upon him—and in such vast numbers, too!

His lordship hesitated, then commanded, "Just be certain to keep them all out of my way."

Perhaps providing him with legitimate employment would keep this cousin from robbing others, his lordship reasoned as he strode from the room. As for the children—well, he did not intend to remain at Penderrick Keep. He supposed he could tolerate them for just a little while.

=FIVE=

"You know I cannot abide the tedious meetings of the Ladies' Society for the Charitable Assistance of the Worthy Poor," Rosamunde complained to Mary Ann. She threw herself back against the pillows of the bed in the room upstairs which they shared.

"'Tis a good cause," Mary Ann quietly reminded her.

"You know I cannot abide the Misses Randolph, either."

"But . . . but they are well-intentioned ladies."

"Yes," Rosamunde conceded, nodding. Still and all, what a great pity that, in the Misses Randolph, good intentions need be accompanied by tediousness.

"Do you not think it kind of them to offer their home every Thursday afternoon so that the ladies of the parish can collect clothing for the improvement of the poor?"

"If they wish to improve the poor, they may begin with us," Rosamunde muttered to herself.

"Oh, do have a care, Dudley," Mrs. Wickes' strident voice echoed up the stairwell and into the girls' bedchamber.

"'Tis not something I do by choice, ye cantankerous fishwife."

Rosamunde thought Uncle Peg's response not only lacked its usual quickness, but also the edge which came to his voice when he was verbally sparring with his sister-in-law.

Rosamunde sprang from the bed and rapidly descended the staircase. She had just reached the bottom step and

51

turned to enter the sitting room when she caught sight of Uncle Peg stumbling across the carpet before coming to rest in his customary chair.

"Uncle Peg, what happened?" she exclaimed, rushing to his side.

"He insists upon dragging that . . . that awful piece of wood across my carpet," Mrs. Wickes complained, gesturing disdainfully at the peg.

Rosamunde frowned with a sense of impending trouble. "You've never dragged that leg before," she whispered to her uncle.

"It . . . it only began yesterday evening," he reluctantly admitted in a voice so weak that she was forced to bend her left ear closer to hear him clearly. "After Lord Merritt and Mr. Whitlaw left."

As he settled himself in his chair, Rosamunde also noted that his left arm appeared unaccountably limp and that he held the fingers of that hand in a cramped curl.

Rosamunde stared at the floor. She did not want Uncle Peg to see the deep concern in her eyes. Apparently his attack yesterday was more serious than they had at first supposed.

"The carpet is already threadbare," Mrs. Wickes continued to complain. "Must you make it worse?"

"I do not think any deliberate malice is intended, Stepmama," Rosamunde tried to reason with her.

"Deliberate or not, splinters from that leg are bound to snag and tear the carpet," Mrs. Wickes grumbled. "We certainly cannot afford to buy another, and I am not about to go to all the trouble of rearranging the furniture just to cover any *new* holes he may make."

Rosamunde realized there would be no reasoning with Stepmama today. She turned to Uncle Peg. "Well, now that you have made it to your chair, why don't you let me bring you a book, and you and I can read this afternoon?" she suggested.

"But, Rosamunde," Mary Ann pouted from the doorway.

"I thought you and I were calling upon the Misses Randolph this afternoon."

"Oh, dear. I'm sorry, Uncle Peg," Rosamunde said with a sigh. "I'm afraid our reading will have to wait."

Rosamunde cast Mary Ann a disparaging glance. She greatly doubted that Mary Ann would even have the courage to go to Heaven unless Rosamunde accompanied her.

"Whyever should you be going out?" Mrs. Wickes demanded. "Why, Lord Merritt may decide at any time to call again unexpectedly."

Rosamunde did not think his lordship would be calling upon this poor, insignificant corner of Penzance ever again, no matter how much polite interest he had feigned in Uncle Peg's sea tales. Why, she marveled that his haughty lordship had ever deigned to call in the first place.

He had probably come because he had heard people talking of Peg as something of a local curiosity. Having no better occupation with which to while away his hours in Penzance, he had decided to seek out Peg for whatever entertainment he might provide.

Well, she certainly hoped his lordship was satisfied. Still, she paused to reflect, he had seemed so concerned about Uncle Peg . . .

"But, Mama, Mr. Shelby will be there as well," Mary Ann timidly reminded her mother.

"Oh, indeed?" Mrs. Wickes' face brightened as she turned to her stepdaughter. "Then you *must* go."

Rosamunde made no effort to conceal her grimace.

"Rosamunde, you have been *most* uncooperative in this matter," Mrs. Wickes scolded. "Mr. Shelby may be merely a country vicar, but he is not an altogether undesirable match."

Even though she was quite certain her stepmother was not paying her any heed, Rosamunde felt compelled to say, "But, Stepmama, I do not think he wants to marry me."

"Why, he does. He must," Mrs. Wickes insisted. "Why else would he continue to call here?"

Rosamunde shrugged. She did not think Stepmama would take kindly to the suggestion that perhaps it was not Rosamunde but the sandwiches which attracted Mr. Shelby.

"'Tis simply not proper," Miss Sophie Randolph pronounced. With her forefinger, she poked her spectacles higher upon her aquiline nose.

"Quite right," Miss Sarah Randolph agreed. She peered at her sister from over the top of the spectacles which perched low on her own long nose.

"A vicar should be married," Miss Sophie continued, "in order to provide the parish with a good example of familial happiness and marital harmony."

"Since Mr. Shelby came to us in a single state, 'tis our duty to assist him in finding a wife so that he can provide that good example," Miss Sarah declared. "I have decided upon an excellent match."

At last! Some interesting conversation, Rosamunde decided. She glanced from Miss Sarah to Miss Sophie, whose spectacles were again slipping down her long nose. She was heartily weary of hearing these ladies complain of the lamentable condition of the poor in faraway lands. Certainly, Rosamunde was sympathetic to their plight and did what she could to help. On the other hand, she would much rather hear tales of exciting adventures in these same faraway lands.

"Who have you chosen for Mr. Shelby?" the Widow Camberton inquired.

"Why, Jane Pendleton," Miss Sarah announced. "A more sensible, industrious lady you will never find. There simply is no other logical choice."

"Why, she's much too old," Mary Ann protested.

Rosamunde turned quickly to her stepsister. These were the first words she had heard the girl utter since their arrival.

Not only that, Mary Ann was actually voicing a dissenting opinion!

"But . . ."

"No," Mary Ann interrupted Miss Sarah. She shook her head emphatically. "She's too old to bear healthy children. Then where would your fine example of familial happiness be?"

"Well . . ." Miss Sarah retreated.

"There is Harriette Morley," the Widow Camberton offered. "Much younger . . ."

"And barely able to cipher two and two," Mary Ann said. "How can a vicar serve his parish well if his wife hasn't the intellect to maintain her household accounts properly?"

"Well. . . ." the Widow Camberton also retreated.

"Cecily Waters is neither too old nor too bird-witted," Mrs. Thwaitesbury asserted. "And rather pretty, as well."

"Indeed, a prime choice, Agnes," Miss Sarah agreed, readily switching allegiances.

"Have you never asked yourselves why a lady of such a suitable age, and intellect, and countenance is not already married?" Mary Ann demanded. "Have you never heard her swearing at their housemaid?"

"No!" the Widow Camberton exclaimed, placing her hand upon her withered breast. "Swearing?"

"Like a very fishwife," Mary Ann said, nodding her head emphatically. "How would that suit your ideal of marital harmony?"

"Then perhaps Rosamunde . . ." the Widow Camberton began with a little laugh.

"I have no intention of marrying Mr. Shelby," Rosamunde asserted.

The ladies looked at her, aghast.

"Oh, do not misunderstand me," she hastened to explain. "Mr. Shelby is quite pleasant. 'Tis just I have no intention of marrying anyone."

The ladies looked at her as if she were quite mad.

"Then there is no one left," Miss Sophie lamented.

"No one but you, Mary Ann," Miss Sarah suggested.

"I?" Mary Ann asked.

She appeared wide-eyed with surprise, yet Rosamunde noted the small smile which played about her stepsister's rosy little lips and the faint blush which colored her porcelain cheeks.

Miss Sophie adjusted her spectacles higher upon her nose and examined Mary Ann. Miss Sarah pushed her spectacles farther down her nose, the better to view Mary Ann over the top of them.

"She *is* the proper age," Miss Sophie observed.

"Comely enough," the Widow Camberton added.

"Pleasant enough," Miss Sarah concurred.

"I have *never* heard her swear," Rosamunde attested with a grin.

"Why, how . . . how flattering that you all should think of me as . . . as suitable to be the vicar's wife," Mary Ann said.

Rosamunde was more intent upon noting that while her shy stepsister had stammered and blushed at the mention of her name as a proposed wife for the vicar, at no time did Mary Ann ever emphatically deny the possibility.

Mary Ann sighed aloud. "However, the choice truly is Mr. Shelby's, is it not?"

The ladies sighed in unison. How unfortunate, they all agreed, that in spite of a lady's machinations, usually the choice, and certainly the initiative, did rest with the gentleman. They lapsed into silent contemplation of the inequities of life.

"Good afternoon, ladies," the masculine voice intruded, not unwelcomed, upon the feminine conclave.

"Mr. Shelby, how good of you to join us," Miss Sophie said, bustling up to him.

"Won't you have a seat, Mr. Shelby?" the Widow Camberton said, indicating the empty chair beside her.

"No, thank you," Mr. Shelby said, waving his hand

before him. "I've merely come to give my sanction to your charitable endeavor. There are a few other calls I must yet make."

"We have some delicious cakes and tea," Miss Sarah said. "Won't you at least stay long enough to try them?"

"Ah, well, perhaps just half a cup," Mr. Shelby quickly agreed, his doleful brown eyes lighting up. "And maybe a cake . . . or two."

The vicar squeezed himself onto the sofa, between Mrs. Thwaitesbury and Mary Ann.

"Why, we were just speaking of you," the Widow Camberton said. She winked knowingly at Mary Ann.

"I do hope you were not commenting unfavorably upon my last Sunday's sermon," he replied with a grin.

"I found it greatly inspiring," Miss Sarah exclaimed, clasping her hands to her bosom and raising her eyes heavenward over her spectacles.

"I hope you found it likewise, Miss Bellows," Mr. Shelby said, turning to Mary Ann.

Mary Ann smiled shyly, barely daring to look in his direction. She silently nodded.

Rosamunde sighed with despair. It was quite evident to her that Mary Ann liked Mr. Shelby. How on earth did her exceptionally timid stepsister ever hope to gain his notice if she never spoke to him?

Rosamunde was quite amazed when Lord Merritt and Mr. Whitlaw called again at Eglantine Cottage the very next day.

"Oh, we are ever so flattered, my lord!" Mrs. Wickes gushed as she escorted Lord Merritt into the sitting room. She left Mr. Whitlaw to trail along behind.

As Mr. Whitlaw prepared to seat himself beside Mary Ann on the threadbare blue damask sofa, Mrs. Wickes grasped his elbow and guided him to one of the equally threadbare chairs situated to the opposite side of the table.

"I'm sure you'll find it much easier to reach the cakes from here," she said.

"Lord Merritt, if you please," Mrs. Wickes said, indicating the very same seat from which she had so recently evicted Mr. Whitlaw.

"Stepmama, his lordship will also be unable to reach the cakes from there," Rosamunde could not resist pointing out. Behind her, she heard Uncle Peg chuckle.

"Oh, Mary Ann will be pleased to serve his lordship," Mrs. Wickes answered readily. "Won't you, Mary Ann?"

Mary Ann silently nodded.

Oh well, of course Mary Ann would agree to anything Stepmama said, Rosamunde decided. That could be the only reason why her stepsister so readily complied. She could not possibly have any other interest in the aloof Lord Merritt. Why, who could?

Mrs. Wickes took the seat beside Mr. Whitlaw. As usual, Rosamunde was left to see to her own comfort. She found a place on the small chair against the wall behind Uncle Peg.

Rosamunde watched Lord Merritt take his place beside Mary Ann. She marveled that the man could sit so erect. He held his head at such a haughty angle, too, as if those icy blue eyes peered down that fine, straight nose of his with utter disdain for all they surveyed.

Where, she allowed herself to wonder, was the man in whose eyes she had once seen such concern for her aged uncle and—dare she think it, for her as well?

"How do you find Penderrick Keep, my lord?" Mrs. Wickes asked. She handed a cup to Mary Ann to pass to his lordship.

" 'Tis adequate," his lordship responded.

"It appears to be *such* a fine place." Mrs. Wickes, undaunted by Lord Merritt's reticence, made another attempt at conversation. "From what little I have seen from the *outside*."

" 'Tis conveniently designed," Lord Merritt reluctantly agreed.

"I should think it a fine place to raise a family," Mrs. Wickes continued.

Rosamunde cringed.

"I shall never find out, as I intend to sell Penderrick Keep."

"Soon?" Mrs. Wickes exclaimed.

Rosamunde thought Stepmama's eyes would pop out of her head with shock and dismay.

"In the near future," Lord Merritt replied.

"But . . . but the gardens and park appear so delightful," Mrs. Wickes said.

"Indeed. I made a brief tour of the estates this morning."

"Avast!" Sir Polly squawked. He flapped his multicolored wings and pivoted on the back of Uncle Peg's chair. "Hard to port! Heave to, ye maggot-ridden swab!"

Rosamunde watched with a certain amount of justified glee as it was now Stepmama's turn to cringe.

"Beware, m'lord," Peg said.

Rosamunde saw Lord Merritt's icy blue eyes suddenly sparkle as he turned to Peg.

"Beware?" his lordship repeated slowly. "Of what have I to beware?"

"Beware the mines, m'lord," Peg continued. "Along the march of our two lands, there be the shafts o' tin mines, abandoned as their ore was exhausted, yet they were never closed."

"How intriguing!" Roger exclaimed. "Do you suppose we could mount an expedition to explore the mines, take a picnic. 'Twould be great adventure."

"Belay that bilge!" Sir Polly screeched.

"Nay, 'tis not a place to be going for diversions," Peg insisted, shaking his head. "A person could tumble down a shaft and never be heard from again."

"Surely if we were all together," Roger offered.

"Not even then."

"Why not?" Lord Merritt asked.

"The place be riddled with mine shafts, tunnels, and caves that go on endlessly," Peg explained. " 'Tis a bad place to be lost."

"Or a good place to be hidden," Lord Merritt countered, his blue eyes narrowing.

"Aye, that, too," Peg agreed. "If a person has a mind to be hid."

"Or a mind to hide something, perhaps?" Lord Merritt suggested. "Tell us, Peg, do you know any tales of hidden—"

"I know naught o' hidden things," Peg said quickly. The furrows of his weathered brow deepened.

"Surely an old seaman such as yourself has heard—"

"Tales. Naught but tales," Peg said, making a gesture of dismissal with his good hand.

"Could you not remember even one for us now?" Lord Merritt persisted.

Rosamunde frowned. Why had Lord Merritt suddenly become so animated at the mere mention of hidden treasure? Why was Lord Merritt so insistent upon hearing any of Uncle Peg's tales regarding such? She watched him intently. What was the man about?

She surveyed the shabby sitting room with its threadbare furniture, worn carpet, and faded wallpaper. Silently, she gave a rueful little chuckle. Just look at this place! Lord Merritt might be foolish enough to believe Uncle Peg's claims to have once been a pirate, but how could the man possibly suppose Uncle Peg had hidden treasure?

She looked at Lord Merritt in his superbly fitting jacket and impeccably styled, skintight pantaloons. What reason, beyond pure greed, could anyone as wealthy as his lordship have in seeking *their* treasure—even *if* they had one!

"Ah," Peg exclaimed, his face suddenly brightening, "I will tell ye a tale o' *sunken* treasure."

"Have another cake, my lord," Mrs. Wickes invited in

what Rosamunde knew was her usual bid to detract attention from Uncle Peg and his sea tales.

"Was it a large treasure?" Roger asked eagerly, apparently not susceptible to Mrs. Wickes' distractions.

"Aye. As large and rich as an entire town," Peg said.

"Now I am certain you are jesting," Lord Merritt asserted.

Peg nodded his head most emphatically. "It be that large when the treasure *is* the entire town."

"Shall I refresh your tea . . . ?"

"A sunken town?" Lord Merritt asked, blatantly ignoring Mrs. Wickes.

Peg grinned broadly and began his tale.

"Me mates and I were partaking of a bit o' rum at the 'Virgin's Delight,' a friendly type of inn where an old sea dog might down a jug or two o' rum without having to worry about getting himself run through, if ye take me meaning."

All the while she listened to Uncle Peg's tale, Rosamunde watched Lord Merritt as he, too, listened.

The skepticism slowly disappeared from his lordship's icy blue eyes. The man was leaning forward in his seat, his elbows resting upon his knees. Through the fabric of his jacket, Rosamunde could see that the muscles of his long back, rather than ramrod straight, were sloping in a gentle arc.

His lordship actually appeared to be at ease, Rosamunde thought. For the first time since she'd met him, he actually appeared to be enjoying himself. The grin on his face had widened to a smile.

'Why, the man is actually *quite* handsome,' she decided, 'on the rare occasions when he deigns to smile.'

"We were making merry," Peg recounted. "It took more than the shaking o' the earth to bother old sailors used to the heaving waves beneath our feet. But then the sky turned an unnatural yellow, and the sea became like glass and began to retreat."

" 'Twas merely the tide going out," Lord Merritt protested.

"Aye, she went out," Peg agreed. "Farther out than ever before, and not at the proper time o' day, either."

Peg's voice was deep and he spoke slowly. "When the tide returned, she came in a rush, as if she'd sorely missed the land, being gone so long. The sea poured in, covering ships at anchor with all their cargo laden down. Then it swallowed up the waterfront, inns, shops—and all those luckless souls who hadn't fled upland."

"But you escaped," Rosamunde prompted.

Peg nodded gravely. "Aye, I fled to the hills, but many a pirate, bold and daring, lies beneath the sea, not to mention a city's worth o' treasure there for the fishes for all eternity."

"Port Royal!" Lord Merritt exclaimed. " 'Twas Port Royal that sank in an earthquake." The smile left his lips, his back stiffened, and his cold, blue eyes narrowed. "In 1692!"

"Quite correct," Peg said. "How good to know ye too remember."

" 'Twould be impossible for you to have been there. No one could be that old!"

Peg shrugged his bony shoulders and grinned slyly. "Ah, well, time passes quickly at sea."

Roger began to laugh. "Oh, come now, Merritt. Do you actually give the tale credence? 'Tis a clever diversion, nothing more."

Rosamunde frowned. Why was Lord Merritt so upset? *No one* ever took Uncle Peg seriously!

"*Now* might I refresh your tea, m'lord?" Mrs. Wickes asked.

Lord Merritt nodded his acceptance of Mrs. Wickes' offer.

Rosamunde rose and retrieved Uncle Peg's cup to supply him with a much-needed drink after his recounting of the tale. She moved toward the table and stood beside Mr.

Whitlaw. She placed several cakes upon Uncle Peg's saucer.

"Rosamunde!" Mrs. Wickes scolded quite loudly. "How can you be so rude to Mr. Whitlaw when he is speaking to you?"

Rosamunde quickly straightened. A deep flush flooded her pale cheeks.

"Oh, I do beg your pardon," she said, turning directly to face Mr. Whitlaw in case he should say more.

She had not heard him. Oh, why did Stepmama have to embarrass her so in the presence of their callers, especially the haughty Lord Merritt!

" 'Twas a trivial request for another cake," Mr. Whitlaw said, his face almost as crimson as Rosamunde's. "It hardly bears repeating."

"Please forgive me," Rosamunde said. She handed him the troublesome cake and quickly retreated to her chair in the corner, the better to hide her embarrassment.

When, at length, she ventured to look up, much to her chagrin, she met Lord Merritt's silver-blue eyes regarding her closely.

She frowned and lowered her gaze. Did his lofty lordship intend to add his censure to Stepmama's?

She peeked up again. My gracious! Lord Merritt was *still* watching her, with an expression less of censure than of curiosity.

Well, fie on his lordship if he thought that she, like her uncle, was merely an object for his entertainment while he was stranded in Penzance! She had no intention of being any man's entertainment—no matter how handsome he might be.

After Lord Merritt and Mr. Whitlaw departed, Rosamunde alone remained to clear away the tea.

"Almost caught you out that time, didn't she?" Uncle Peg asked.

"What . . . what do you mean?" Rosamunde stammered.

"You needn't dissemble before your old Uncle Peg. How long have you been deaf in your right ear?"

Rosamunde flushed to the roots of her dark hair. "Oh, I'm not . . . well, just a bit . . . oh, dear, and I thought I had managed to hide it so well all these years," she finally admitted. "How could you tell?"

"I'm old and crippled," Uncle Peg told her with a little chuckle. "But I'm not stupid."

Rosamunde slowly returned her uncle's smile.

"I've seen how you miss what people say when they are standing to your right, and how you turn your head when someone speaks to you."

Rosamunde nodded, a worried look upon her face. "Do you think anyone else has noticed?"

"What if they have? 'Tis no shame," Peg reassured her. "How did it happen? Were you born deaf in that ear?"

"No. 'Twas a careless shooting accident," she admitted. "I was but ten or eleven. Cousin Fenton and I were playing by the shooting party's guns. I had no idea he would actually fire one of them. I was standing too close when he did. My ear rang horribly for almost a week, and since then I've never heard another thing with it. I never complained of my injury for fear that Fenton should find himself in more trouble than he already was."

"You were more noble than Fenton deserved," Peg remarked sarcastically.

"There really was nothing to be done for it anyway," she said with a resigned shrug. "You . . . you won't tell anyone, will you?"

"Rosamunde!" Peg declared in a very injured tone of voice. "How can you even think that I would tell? Haven't I kept your secret this long?"

She nodded, abashed.

"Anyway, you and I, we must stand together, mustn't we?"

She smiled and nodded again.

"After all, my dear," he said, patting his pegged leg with his good hand, "lately, 'tis becoming deucedly difficult for me to stand on my own."

=SIX=

"Merritt, I have heard of robbers entering one's home and departing with the contents," Roger said when they returned to Penderrick Keep late that afternoon. "I have *never* heard of robbers *leaving* furniture."

Lord Merritt, struggling to keep the shock from showing on his face, peered at the strange bench which now graced his hall opposite the table. He approached it, held out his hand and touched it.

" 'Tis real enough," Roger commented. With a laugh, he dropped himself onto the bench. A rear leg collapsed, sending him sprawling to the floor. Springing to his feet, Roger laughed once more.

"He's not quite finished with that yet, m'lord," Fickle said.

"He?" Lord Merritt asked.

"My sister's husband, m'lord," Fickle explained. "He's an excellent carpenter. Would you believe he found that in the barn?"

Lord Merritt inspected more closely the roughly finished wood and poorly turned legs and spindles of the back.

"Indeed, I would," he answered. What in the world was Fickle's brother-in-law doing in the barn with old Penderrick furniture?

"You see, m'lord," Fickle continued, "I figured that if your lordship was going to all the trouble to have the gardens tended and the rooms cleaned, well, mightn't it be a good idea to put some furnishings in these rooms?"

"But there is no furniture left at Penderrick Keep," Lord Merritt protested.

"Indeed there is, in the cellars and attics and outbuildings," Fickle pointed out.

"And your brother-in-law is the very man who can repair all this furniture—for a reasonable sum, of course?"

"Ah, you've a ready mind, m'lord."

"I suppose he and all his brood will be descending upon Penderrick Keep," Lord Merritt asked, already resigned to his fate.

"No, m'lord. They have no children."

Lord Merritt breathed a sigh of relief and headed for the stairs to go to his room to change for dinner.

"Their first child is not due for another two weeks."

A woman *enceinte*! An infant! Here? Lord Merritt stopped in his tracks. He could only hope that, in another two weeks, he would ascertain the truth of the lost Penderrick fortune and be gone from Penderrick Keep.

"Fickle," Lord Merritt said, turning to his audacious butler. He tried not to grin. "How much longer before your entire family is employed here?"

"I've a large family, m'lord."

His lordship turned and, with a slow, resigned shake of his head, continued up the stairs. "That is precisely what I was afraid you would say."

"The housemaid's apologies, m'lord," Fickle said. "The dining room remains unfinished."

"'Tis no matter, Fickle," Lord Merritt replied. "If your mother prepares as good a dinner as she did a breakfast, I shan't mind where 'tis served."

Lord Merritt blinked in bewilderment when he realized what he had just said. It always *used* to matter a great deal to him precisely where and how dinner, and every meal, was served. It always *used* to be very important to him that all the furnishings be precisely designed and arranged to bring out the perfect proportions of each room in all his residences.

This unusual part of the country and its equally unusual inhabitants were having a strange effect upon him. Was this good or bad? He could not be certain.

Lord Merritt was certain, however, that dinner was as excellent as he had expected. Mrs. Fickle prepared a creamy chicken broth, baked turbot, and a roasted leg of salt pork with tart applesauce—simple, country fare, but he was finding it thoroughly delightful.

He was about to take up one more piece of the tender meat when a hard, round object rolled across the table to settle directly on his plate.

"Roger, there appears to be a cricket ball in my applesauce," his lordship observed.

Roger emitted an injured sniff. "What wretched hospitality! *I* was not served one. Tell me, Merritt, do you prefer them baked or boiled?"

"Neither—"

"Oh, don't tell me you eat them raw," Roger exclaimed. "How barbaric!"

"Begging your lordship's pardon," came the small voice from the doorway.

Lord Merritt looked up. How had Fickle managed to shrink?

"Might I have my ball back?" the minuscule image of his butler asked.

"You may," Roger answered, gesturing for the small boy to enter the drawing room. "His lordship prefers his prepared in a different fashion."

The boy frowned and looked at Roger as if he considered him quite mad. Indeed, Lord Merritt was in hearty agreement with the lad.

"Who are you?" his lordship demanded.

"Terrence, m'lord."

"Where did you come from, Terrence?" his lordship asked a bit more gently.

"Penzance, m'lord."

"No, I mean—"

"He's my youngest brother, m'lord," Fickle said, rushing to his lordship's side.

"How could I ever doubt it?" Lord Merritt replied.

With his thumb and forefinger, the butler gingerly lifted the cricket ball from his lordship's plate. He wiped the applesauce from the ball with the edge of the linen tablecloth. Bending down to his brother, he whispered crossly, "Now, begone with you. And don't let this happen again!"

Retrieving his ball, Terrence scampered from the room.

"Isn't your brother a bit young to be employed here, Fickle?"

"With my mother here, m'lord, there's no one home to mind the younger children," Fickle explained.

"Is there no aunt?"

"She's here, too, m'lord. Remember?"

Lord Merritt nodded silently. "Fickle, by any chance is this the same aunt who was suspected of consorting with . . . ?"

"Indeed not, m'lord!" Fickle exclaimed. "That one was transported years ago."

"Thank you, Fickle. I feel much reassured."

Then Lord Merritt raised his head and tried to give his butler his most commanding glare. "Fickle, if your family is to remain here, I insist the children be kept from underfoot—*and* out of my dinner! Do I make myself clear?"

Lord Merritt had no intention of allowing the man to think that just because he had, in a moment of magnanimity, consented to employ certain members of the family, he would allow the entire clan to take up residence here—and overrun the place!

Lord Merritt sat in the quiet of the gathering darkness. Fickle had cleared away dinner, but had not yet returned to light the candles for the evening. The excellent meal had rendered Roger quite somnolent—and blissfully silent for a change.

He swirled his amber brandy in its snifter, then lifted it to the waning light which shone through the tall windows. A large shadow blotted out the light.

Looking up, Lord Merritt was confronted by the forms of the hulking Gidley and the furtive Raikes. Lord Merritt darted a quick glance to Roger, who was snoring quite loudly in his chair.

"Good evening, m'lord," Raikes said, bowing low.

Lord Merritt stiffened his spine and stared the man coldly in the eye. The muscles of his legs and shoulders tensed, preparing for whatever action he might need take. "A rather unexpected call, wouldn't you say?" he asked.

"Begging yer lordship's pardon," Raikes continued, bowing once again. "Surely ye understand our rather pressing concern for the rapid discovery o' the location o' this fortune."

His lordship continued his icy stare at the wiry little man. "Surely *you* understand my dislike of being disturbed at such an hour and in such a manner."

"Yer lordship would be even more disturbed if Dudley Wickes died before disclosing his secret," Raikes countered.

The same thought had once occurred to Lord Merritt. Now, regardless of how likable he thought the old fellow, he merely believed Dudley Wickes a clever weaver of tales, and perhaps not even altogether sane.

However, Lord Merritt was never in the habit of making others privy to his thoughts. He merely shrugged. "I have lived this long without the knowledge," he answered noncommittally.

"Methinks I've lived even longer, m'lord, and *I* grow weary o' waiting," Raikes answered. "Might I remind yer lordship that Dudley Wickes is not a well man."

Lord Merritt could not refute that statement. He had seen with his own eyes that Peg was ill and aged beyond his years.

His fine lips tightened and the muscles of his squared jaw

clenched. The callous bastards! How dare they insist he badger a sick old man!

"You placed this matter in my hands," Lord Merritt informed them, rising to his feet with great dignity. "Now I will deal with it as *I* see fit."

He took a step toward them both.

"And *you* will simply have to wait."

Slowly, he strode toward one of the long windows which opened to what was once the garden and gestured outward.

"You will leave in the same skulking manner by which I assume you entered," he commanded. "You will only return here *when* and *if* I summon you."

Raikes nodded and bowed low. Tapping the arm of his companion, he headed for the door. He turned. Raising his index finger, he warned, "Do not be wasting time, m'lord. 'Tis almost as precious as the gold ye seek."

The two men faded into the twilight.

"Oh, I say, Merritt," Roger's disappointed call came from his chair. "Does this mean the deal with Raikes and that gruesome Gidley fellow is off?"

"There is no deal with Raikes," Lord Merritt answered as he settled glumly into his chair. "The man is a greedy opportunist. Dudley Wickes is in his dotage, and we are all just as mad as March hares if we believe the preposterous tales that he tells are actually true."

"Ah, well then, I suppose there is no need to return to Eglantine Cottage," Roger remarked with a theatrically heavy sigh.

"I . . . I did not say that," Lord Merritt said slowly. "I merely said that we may hope for no sensible information from Peg." He raised his snifter and took a sip of brandy. "Actually, I rather like the old fellow and his outlandish tales. We may still pay him a call." Trying very hard to sound casual, he added, "Occasionally."

Roger nodded sagely.

"Merely to pass the time, of course," Lord Merritt

expanded his explanation. "After all, there truly is little else
to do here."

"Very little," Roger concurred.

"And the old man's tales *are* highly entertaining."

"Oh, 'tis highly entertaining to visit Eglantine Cottage,"
Roger agreed.

'Twas not only entertaining to visit Eglantine Cottage,
Lord Merritt mused, 'twas downright intriguing. Oh, not
just because of Peg's tales, although they were interesting,
but Miss Rosamunde Wickes also piqued his curiosity.

She had a way about her of comforting the sick old man,
and, at the same time, of prodding his mind—or at least
what was left of it—to greater activity.

She was a puzzlement to him, too. She appeared to have
quite a lively sense of humor and an active mind herself.
Why, then, had she ignored Roger's small request? He
surmised from her stepmother's reaction that this was not
the first time something like this had happened.

Lord Merritt decided that a return visit, or perhaps even
several visits, to Eglantine Cottage might not be out of
place. Even if no missing fortune were forthcoming from
the excursions, perhaps he could discover more about the
unusual Miss Wickes.

Rosamunde had never heard such an uproar! She sat up
quickly and tossed the coverlet aside. Grabbing her wrapper, she made for the door.

"Oh, Rosamunde! Do you think you should go down
there?" Mary Ann cried, her blue eyes wide with fright. She
was still in the bed, the coverlet pulled close up to her chin.

"'Tis Uncle Peg. I can hear Sir Polly, too." Rosamunde
shook her head. "I fear something dreadful is afoot."

"If you must go, do close the door after you," Mary Ann
pleaded.

"Will you have the courage to remove yourself from that
bed and lock it behind me?" Rosamunde asked sarcastically
as she left her cowardly stepsister behind.

She followed the raucous, angry sounds to the small room at the side of the house which Mrs. Wickes had reluctantly designated for Peg's use.

"Where is it, ye coldhearted harpy?" Peg shouted. "What have ye done with it? The same as ye did with me broadsword, I'll wager!"

Rosamunde shouldered her way between her father and her stepmother, who were obstructing the doorway. "Step-mama took your broadsword years ago, Uncle Peg," she said. "What is missing now?" She stopped abruptly at the foot of his bed.

The wooden peg, which for five years had rested against the wall at the head of his bed when he removed it each night, was no longer there.

Rosamunde whirled to her stepmother. "What have you done with it?" she demanded.

"I?" Mrs. Wickes asked, glaring haughtily at Rosamunde as if highly affronted.

"I do not think Sir Polly carried it off."

" 'Twouldn't fit him, anyway," Peg muttered from his bed.

"Yes, I took it," Mrs. Wickes boldly confessed. "I came in the middle of the night and took that wretched thing."

"How could you be so cruel?" Rosamunde cried.

"I am not cruel. I am practical," Mrs. Wickes maintained. "Yesterday evening, I found another hole in the carpet, so large that I shall have to rearrange the furniture in order to hide it. I determined then and there never again to allow Dudley to destroy the few pitiful possessions I still have."

"Return it to me, ye baboon-faced trollop!" Peg demanded.

Mrs. Wickes folded her large arms over her ample breasts and looked away.

"I wasn't quite as attached to the thing as I was to my original leg," Peg admitted, "but I have grown rather accustomed to it. Return it to me this instant!"

"I cannot."

"Cannot or will not?"

"I *can* not," Mrs. Wicks elaborated. "I burned it."

Rosamunde's mouth dropped open, attesting to her surprise and horror.

"I asked you many times, Dudley, to have a care," Mrs. Wickes said, shaking her head slowly. "But you chose to ignore me. I warned you that you would be sorry. So there you are. Now it is gone—and you've only yourself to blame." Mrs. Wickes gave one last, decisive nod of her head. "Now, if I could only rid myself of that wretched parrot," she said, "I could put an end once and for all to your piratical delusions."

Peg began to laugh.

Mrs. Wickes startled at the unexpected sound. She eyed him cautiously. Then her frown deepened. "Now I know you are truly mad, Dudley."

"Oh, no, Catherine," Peg denied between laughs. "I am quite sane."

Mrs. Wickes' face was so red that Rosamunde believed that, at any moment, her head might go shooting off like a Roman candle.

"'Tis justice, Catherine," Peg said with another hearty laugh. "Justice, pure and simple."

Mrs. Wickes glared at him. "Indeed. There is justice in not having my carpet further ruined."

"No," Peg said, shaking his head. "Ye did this to make me sorry, and, in truth, I am—just a bit. But in the end, ye'll regret this more than I ever shall."

Mrs. Wickes stared at him in bewilderment.

"Ye'll see," he repeated, still chuckling. "Ye *will* be sorry."

Rosamunde regarded Uncle Peg. After five years, she knew him well enough to know that he never made a promise, never made a threat, that he didn't carry out. She wished she knew what he had planned this time.

• • •

Raikes took a long draught of his ale, then set the mug on the rough-hewn table before him. He stared directly at Gidley, who was seated across the table from him at the Dead Man's Head Inn.

"Methinks we've been mistaken, Gidley," he said, shaking his head.

Gidley cocked his head and raised one heavy eyebrow.

"We never should've trusted Lord Merritt."

Gidley frowned questioningly.

"Suppose he informs the constable about us?" Raikes demanded.

Gidley shook his head.

"Ye think not, eh?" Raikes asked, regarding his silent companion. "Well, I suppose ye could be right. I doubt his lordship'd be wanting it known he was party to a bit of a havy-cavy affair."

Gidley nodded.

"But suppose he's already got the information from Peg? Suppose he's already found the treasure and has decided to cheat us out of our fair share?"

Again Gidley shook his head.

"Well, and why not?" Raikes demanded sharply.

Gidley silently continued to shake his head.

"Bloody hell, what a nuisance ye are!" Raikes exclaimed. "I wish that sot of a hangman had done a proper job and killed ye outright instead o' just ruining yer voice box."

Gidley nodded, a wry grimace twisting his lips.

"What makes ye think his lordship hasn't yet found it?" Raikes repeated.

Gidley jerked his head toward the doorway.

Raikes' dark expression brightened as he at last comprehended the significance of Gidley's gesture. "Indeed. 'Tis for certain, if his lordship had found what we all seek, he'd be well on his way back to London this very minute."

Gidley smiled and nodded.

"Still and all," Raikes grumbled, "I'd feel more reassured keeping an eye on his lordship. Everyone knows ye can't trust a landlubber!"

Gidley nodded his silent agreement. Then his heavy brows drew into a frown, and he motioned toward one dark corner of the taproom.

"Eh, what?" Raikes whispered. He slowly turned about.

A lone man sat drinking in the far corner of the room. He was shorter than the average, yet powerfully built. Every so often, he passed his large hand across his brow and over his bald pate.

"Has he been watching us long?" Raikes asked.

Gidley nodded.

"Ever seen him before?"

Gidley shook his head.

"Innkeeper, more rum!" Raikes shouted. He clattered several coins onto the rough wooden tabletop. The innkeeper, jug in hand, hastened to their table.

Raikes slid a coin toward the edge of the table. As the innkeeper reached for it, Gidley grabbed the man's hand.

"Who be that man in the corner?" Raikes demanded.

"I don't know the man," the innkeeper answered. "Ow! Truly I don't," he vowed as Gidley applied further encouragement. At a gesture from Raikes, Gidley finally released him.

The innkeeper backed away rapidly. Then he frowned with concentration. "Yet, somehow, I get the nagging feeling that I *have* seen him before—but it wasn't him."

"What sort o' answer be that?" Raikes demanded angrily.

From a distance, the innkeeper shrugged and responded, "As good an answer as money *can't* buy."

Gidley nodded toward the corner. Raikes turned around again. The unidentified man threw some coins on the table, then left.

"Then again, maybe it was," the innkeeper said. "At the moment, I just can't seem to remember."

=SEVEN=

"More tea, my lord?" Mrs. Wickes asked.

"No, thank you," Lord Merritt answered. He swirled the spoon listlessly around in his cup.

"More tea, Mr. Whitlaw?" Mrs. Wickes asked.

"Thank you, no," Mr. Whitlaw responded. He looked from his teacup to Lord Merritt, as if waiting for some sign. None was forthcoming.

"Another cake, my lord?" Mrs. Wickes offered.

Without a word, Mary Ann held out the small plate.

Lord Merritt merely shook his head in polite refusal.

Rosamunde sighed. She looked from Stepmama to Mary Ann to Lord Merritt to Mr. Whitlaw, all seated in a little circle around the sitting room, as still and silent as Stonehenge.

Oh, this was even *worse* than when the Silent Vicar paid one of his weekly visits, Rosamunde lamented to herself. At least Mr. Shelby made some attempt at conversation, and Mary Ann sometimes responded. But even Mr. Whitlaw was silent now.

'Should I scream?' Rosamunde debated. 'That would cause some sort of excitement, and the ensuing explanation would be a source of conversation, for a while at least.'

"Actually," Lord Merritt began, startling Rosamunde so that her teacup made a delicate little clatter against the saucer, "I was hoping to visit with Peg again."

Mrs. Wickes blinked and stared at his lordship in surprise. "Why, whatever for?"

77

"I . . . I am quite interested in tales of the sea," his lordship explained. "I should enjoy hearing more of the exciting ones he tells."

"Well, you see," Mrs. Wickes stammered, "lately, Dudley has been . . . well, rather indisposed."

"Incapacitated," Rosamunde corrected.

Lord Merritt's icy blue eyes cast her a puzzled glance.

'Oh, why did I have to draw his attention to myself?' Rosamunde silently demanded of herself. With a small shock of surprise, she realized that she was glad she had.

Swallowing hard in spite of herself, she returned his lordship's gaze. "My uncle lost his leg," she explained.

"Miss Wickes, your uncle lost his leg many years ago," Lord Merritt said. "Do you mean to say that he has just now noticed it is missing?"

To her further surprise, Rosamunde saw a teasing smile gleaming in his lordship's customarily frosty eyes. Why, the man had a sense of humor after all! A rather unusual one, too, from all indications. Just the type she appreciated, and so rarely found around here.

"I believe my uncle would be well pleased to see you again, my lord," she said, giving him a tiny grin. "I shall see if I am able to bring him to you."

She rose. Turning to Mary Ann, she whispered, "I shall need your assistance."

"Oh, no. Truly, no," Mary Ann quickly declined.

Grasping her arm, Rosamunde nudged her stepsister to her feet.

"Oh, Rosamunde, this time I must protest." Mary Ann continued her feeble attempt at rebellion as Rosamunde pulled her along.

As soon as they were out of sight of the others, Mary Ann stubbornly stopped and crossed her arms firmly over her breasts. "No, Rosamunde, I shan't."

"Either you help me get Uncle Peg to the sitting room to visit Lord Merritt or . . . or I shall *never* go to those

wretched meetings at the Misses Randolph again!"
Rosamunde threatened.

"But, Rosamunde . . ." Mary Ann whined.

"Never ever!"

Mary Ann's pretty features twisted into a grimace.

Rosamunde seized Mary Ann's hand and drew her into
Peg's bedchamber.

"Uncle Peg, Lord Merritt is most eager to visit with
you," Rosamunde announced.

"His lordship wants to see me?" Peg repeated, sitting
upright in his bed.

"Indeed he does," Rosamunde replied with a nod. She
reached down to straighten his cravat. "Let's make you
presentable."

Peg looked down at his remaining leg, then at the empty
pant leg tucked beneath him. He heaved a deep sigh. "No,
lass," he said sadly. "I cannot have his lordship see me like
this."

"He has come to hear your pirate tales. You needn't a leg
to tell a good story, Uncle Peg."

Rosamunde watched him for what seemed an interminable
ble time. She worried about him. He had eaten very little
yesterday, and had not eaten any breakfast or luncheon
today at all. The sparkle in his laughing eyes was extinguished.

Then suddenly, Peg slapped his hand upon his thigh and
looked up.

"Well, ladies, are we quite prepared?" he asked.

Perhaps this visit from Lord Merritt was fortuitous after
all, Rosamunde decided. She hoped his lordship's desire to
hear more of Peg's favorite stories would help to cheer her
aging uncle.

Peg threw his good arm about Mary Ann's shoulder.
Carefully, Rosamunde placed her arm under Peg's other,
weaker arm. With surprising ease, he rose to his feet. He
tottered there for only a moment.

"Have no fear," Peg reassured them as he regained his

balance. "I've crossed the deck of a brigantine in a tropic gale with a full mug o' rum in me hand, and never spilled a drop! With a little assistance on your part, ladies, I do believe I can cross to me chair by the fireside."

Sir Polly flapped his wings, took off from his perch in the corner, and alighted on Peg's shoulder, directly beside Mary Ann, where he continued to flap furiously.

Mary Ann squealed in terror. Releasing Peg, she fled to the apparent safety of the doorway.

"He only wishes to help, m'dear," Peg told the frightened girl as he struggled to maintain his disrupted equilibrium.

"Come back and help me," Rosamunde scolded as she held tightly to Peg to prevent him from falling.

Peg twisted his head around to the parrot. "Ye'll have to flap harder than that, Sir Polly," he said with a laugh, "if ye wish to get *me* off the ground."

Sir Polly took flight again, swooping out the bedchamber door. As the parrot sailed toward her, Mary Ann screamed and fled.

"Oh, what a coward!" Rosamunde muttered under her breath.

Rosamunde turned to Peg. Tiny beads of perspiration were beginning to glisten upon his forehead and upper lip as he struggled to stand on a single leg.

"There's little I can do, Uncle Peg," she said. "I doubt I've the strength to help you get about by myself."

"I understand, my dear." Peg sighed. "May as well set me down. If his lordship wishes to hear my tales, he'll just have to come to me."

"At a very early age, my father taught me that others come to the Viscounts Merritt," his lordship said from the doorway. "Not vice versa."

Rosamunde was so taken aback to see his lordship resting his lean frame against the doorjamb that she almost dropped Peg.

"Therefore," his lordship continued, entering the bedchamber, "I shall just have to make certain that you come to the sitting room."

Lord Merritt approached Peg and stood to the opposite side from Rosamunde.

"I . . . I greatly appreciate your assistance, my lord," she managed to say in spite of her shock.

In his blue eyes shone the same concern for her uncle that she had seen when his lordship had first called. Apparently, the stern Lord Merritt had not only a sense of humor, but also more tender human emotions within him as well.

Lately, Rosamunde found she was making some rather pleasantly surprising discoveries about the man.

"When I saw Sir Polly enter the living room alone and settle himself upon his customary chair, I suspected that you might need some assistance," his lordship explained. Grinning at Peg, he continued, "When I saw Miss Bellows enter, my suspicions were confirmed."

Peg chuckled.

"How are you feeling today?" his lordship asked.

"As useless as a poker in July," Peg responded with a wry grin.

Rosamunde was relieved to see the old sparkle returning to her uncle's demeanor.

His lordship placed one long arm under Peg's. As he wrapped his arm about the old man's rib cage, his hand brushed against her breast.

She drew back quickly. Once he had placed a hand to her arm, and she felt as if she had been touched by ice. Now she felt as if she had been touched by fire. Even as she automatically withdrew from such sudden, intimate contact, she found herself instinctively wanting to remain close to Lord Merritt.

"I do beg your pardon, Miss Wickes," his lordship said very quietly.

Oh, why had he said that? she lamented. She might have been able to pretend the contact had never taken place, or that his lordship was completely unaware of it. But his acknowledgment only confirmed the reality of what he had done, and she, my gracious . . . she had enjoyed it!

She could not look up into his piercing blue eyes when he was quite so close. Once she had likened his eyes to silvery mirrors. What revealing reflection of herself would she see if she dared to look into them now? She was suddenly extremely hesitant to confront this hidden part of herself.

Unable to meet his gaze, Rosamunde could only nod her acceptance of his lordship's polite apology. Surely the contact had been inadvertent, she told herself. Surely!

"Ye needn't leave all the work to his lordship, Rosamunde," Peg gently chided her.

She shook herself from her contemplation of Lord Merritt. She opened her mouth to speak, but nothing came forth. Somehow, it seemed impossible to explain. She closed her mouth and drew closer to her uncle—and, slowly and very carefully, to Lord Merritt as well.

"Perhaps it will be easier to support your uncle if we link our arms," his lordship suggested.

Rosamunde frowned, uncertain of how to proceed.

Lord Merritt placed his hand upon her shoulder. Realizing his intent, Rosamunde raised her hand to lay it upon his lordship's shoulder. His arm was longer than hers. Her hand only reached to the muscle of his arm between his shoulder and elbow. 'My gracious,' she thought, 'the man's arm is so strong . . . and firm . . . and . . .' Rosamunde quickly shook such thoughts from her head and concentrated upon the task at hand.

Peg's journey to the sitting room was not quite as rapid as Sir Polly's or Mary Ann's had been, yet nevertheless proceeded more smoothly than Rosamunde could have dared hope.

She assisted Peg in arranging his coattails and propping his leg comfortably upon a footstool. She placed his teacup and a few small cakes upon the table at the side of his chair.

"Is there anything else that you want?" she asked.

Peg heaved a heavy sigh. "Ye cannot bring me what I

truly want, my dear," he answered, shaking his head sadly.

Rosamunde winced. "I wish I could get your leg back . . ."

"Nay, lass!" Peg protested, breaking into a chuckle. He threw Lord Merritt a sly wink. "I was thinking of a certain red-haired doxy I once knew in Cherbourg."

"Oh, Uncle Peg, drink your tea," Rosamunde scolded.

She heard Lord Merritt, standing close beside her, chuckle. She felt a light flush rising in her cheeks. Heretofore, she had always managed to ignore Uncle Peg's sometimes suggestive remarks, knowing that he truly meant no harm. But Lord Merritt's presence rendered her suddenly shy. My gracious! How she disliked being thought missish!

She seated herself in the chair behind Peg's. Lord Merritt did not return to the seat Mrs. Wickes had thrust upon him, but leaned casually against the mantelpiece at Peg's other side. Only then did Rosamunde notice that Mr. Shelby had also come to call.

How odd, Rosamunde noted, that Mr. Shelby occupied the seat beside Mary Ann which Lord Merritt had vacated in order to assist her and Uncle Peg. Perhaps Stepmama based her hope for Heaven upon not offending the vicar. Anyone else, she most assuredly would have ejected from that seat.

How equally strange, Rosamunde decided, that the Silent Vicar should call again so soon. The sandwiches were not *that* tasty. The man must be truly famished if he could bear, twice in one week, Stepmama's immense lack of subtlety in matchmaking.

"How kind of you to invite me again," Mr. Shelby said.

"Rosamunde was quite insistent that you be included," Mrs. Wickes said.

"Well, I did not exactly *insist*." Unfortunately, this was the extent of denial which Rosamunde felt she could make and still remain safely within the bounds of propriety by not calling Stepmama a blatant liar.

"Oh, I should have come in any case," he said, and reached for another sandwich.

"Lord Merritt has persuaded Uncle Peg to tell another of his sea tales," Rosamunde said. She grinned with a certain satisfaction. Having to listen to another of Uncle Peg's stories would serve Stepmama right for telling that enormous falsehood concerning the vicar and her.

"How stirring," Mr. Shelby replied with little enthusiasm. He gave a tiny gulp. "I do hope, however, that this tale contains no scenes of decapitation or disembowelment like the ones Mr. Wickes has recounted upon previous visits."

Mr. Shelby glanced to Mary Ann. She peered up at him with her large blue eyes and nodded her agreement.

"But, then, 'twould not be a pirate tale," Peg insisted. "However, since ye've asked so nicely, I'll tell ye a true tale of a brave and noble pirate—"

"A noble pirate? How can that be?" Mr. Whitlaw asked.

"Indeed," Peg replied. He turned to Lord Merritt and asked, "Tell me, m'lord. How do ye think the good Sir Polly entered the peerage?"

"Surely he was not born to it," Lord Merritt replied, eyeing Peg skeptically. "I had assumed 'twas merely a name given in jest."

Peg's eyes narrowed. He lifted his good right hand and pointed a gnarled finger at Lord Merritt. "Ah, there ye be wrong. 'Twas a title granted him, with all due pomp and ceremony, for his loyal service to his sovereign."

Lord Merritt chuckled in anticipation. "Sir Polly is but a parrot. What could he do?"

"I thought ye'd never ask!" Peg began his tale. " 'Twas the summer o' '43—"

"Oh, come now. Not again," Lord Merritt protested. "You have duped us once, trying to pass off as current tales of things which happened so long ago."

Peg fixed his lordship with a stern glare. "Ye know nothing o' parrots, m'lord. They live nigh as long as humans, in some cases, a lot longer, if ye take me meaning."

Peg drew one long, bony finger across his throat.

Mary Ann gasped and clutched at Mr. Shelby's arm. He reached across and patted her hand reassuringly.

Rosamunde silently shook her head in despair. A mere hint of decapitation, and already her timid stepsister was upon the verge of swooning.

" 'Twas the summer o' 1743," Peg continued. "He was just plain Polly then, the loyal companion—for no man can own this bird—o' Wild Jack Marsh, the Terror o' Trinidad, the bravest pirate ever to sail the Spanish Main."

"How brave was he?" Rosamunde prompted readily, as she had heard, and enjoyed, this tale many times before.

"Why, he was so brave, he took on six Spaniards in battle with only his broadsword and a belaying pin at hand." Peg's voice lowered to a whisper which, nevertheless, carried the length of the room. "He was *so brave*, 'tis claimed by some that he married three women at the same time!"

A wide grin spread across his weather-beaten face.

Roger laughed out loud.

Rosamunde looked across to Lord Merritt. His icy blue eyes thawed with his smile. The little creases at the corners of his eyes warmed his face.

"Ah, but there's a price to pay for such fame," Peg cautioned. "Many a man, hoping to make his name and fortune in the islands, challenged Wild Jack. Many men died. Then came Black Luke, a man who had hated Wild Jack for years, a man who aspired to be the Terror o' Trinidad, and who challenged Wild Jack for the right."

"Hang him from the yardarm!" Sir Polly commanded.

"They fought for hours," Peg continued, recounting blow by bloody blow the gruesome battle. "But Wild Jack's age was beginning to take its toll upon his prowess. Just as Black Luke was about to strike the deathblow, Polly, seeing his companion in mortal danger, flew to his defense, beak and claw, and drove the attacker away."

Rosamunde watched Lord Merritt. He leaned against the mantelpiece, a pleased smile upon his face. There was no skeptical frown upon his brow, no angry disbelief. This time he appeared merely to be enjoying the story for what it was—an entertaining yarn.

"That very night aboard his ship, a most solemn ceremony was conducted by Wild Jack Marsh, the acknowledged king o' the pirates. Using his own broadsword, Wild Jack dubbed his brave companion Sir Polly. Regardless o' the diverse company he has kept over the years, *Sir* Polly he remains to this day."

"Bravo!" Roger exclaimed, applauding. "Tell us another."

"Perhaps one a bit less violent," Mr. Shelby suggested. He glanced solicitously toward Mary Ann, whose fair complexion had turned quite green.

"I truly do not think I can abide one more, Uncle Dudley," Mary Ann pleaded.

"Then ye'll have to be the one to leave, lass," Peg informed her. "Ye've two good legs for moving about, and I'm stuck in this damned chair."

"Come, old fellow," Lord Merritt said, approaching Peg. "After recounting such an adventure, I'm sure you feel the need of a breath of fresh air. I know I do."

Peg grinned up at his lordship. "I shall require some assistance, m'lord. And do bring Sir Polly," he asked Rosamunde.

"Oh, Rosamunde, you cannot leave," Mrs. Wickes cried in alarm. "Not when Mr. Shelby has come to call upon you."

"I do not think that is the case," Rosamunde replied.

Almost frantically, Mrs. Wickes offered, "Mary Ann will assist Dudley."

"I think not," Mary Ann protested, eyeing Sir Polly with intense trepidation.

Merciful heavens! Mary Ann had rebelled thrice in the same week? Rosamunde expected next to see the sky come caving in upon them all.

"Truly, I understand Miss Wickes' need to assist her

uncle," Mr. Shelby reassured Mrs. Wickes. "I . . . I should not object to Miss Bellows' company instead."

Mary Ann smiled shyly at Mr. Shelby and nodded her concession to fate.

Rosamunde held out her arm to Sir Polly. He pivoted on the back of the chair, then executed his little sideways walk up her arm to settle comfortably upon her shoulder.

Lord Merritt quite easily helped Peg rise from the chair. He wrapped one of his long arms about Peg's torso and assisted the old man to hobble out the door to the terrace.

Rosamunde felt a flush begin to creep up her cheeks and a sudden flame of realization within her breast. Why, his lordship had been perfectly capable all along of assisting Uncle Peg without any help from her whatsoever! Yet the man had deliberately required her participation in moving Uncle Peg from his bedchamber to the sitting room.

For the sole purpose of touching her? she cautiously questioned herself. Do not be a goose! she answered quite sternly. His lordship could have no more interest in her than she had in him! Very little interest at all. Was there not?

Lord Merritt had accompanied Peg to the stone bench at the far balustrade of the terrace.

"Ah, the effort has exhausted me, I fear," Peg said as she approached. He held out his right arm.

"You tell quite an exciting tale," Rosamunde said, holding out her arm so that Sir Polly could step to Peg's shoulder.

"Yes, I do, don't I," he agreed without any encumbrance from false modesty. Then he heaved a weary sigh. "But now I am tired. I should like nothing—no, not even that redheaded tart from Cherbourg—nothing better than to sit in the sun for a bit."

"Then you shall do just that, Uncle Peg," Rosamunde said, patting his hand.

"However, that's no reason why you and Lord Merritt should not enjoy the gardens," Peg continued. "In fact, I insist you stroll about them. After all, 'twas on my account

that Lord Merritt missed the tour of our garden the first time
he came to call."

Oh, why did Uncle Peg have to say that? Rosamunde
lamented. What a position that put Lord Merritt in! Surely
Uncle Peg wasn't becoming as persistent a matchmaker as
Stepmama.

"I should enjoy that, if you would consent, Miss
Wickes." With a slight bow, Lord Merritt offered her his
arm.

Rosamunde hesitated. The prospect of strolling about the
garden with Lord Merritt caused a certain quivering inside.
Spending more time with him—*alone* with him—to discover more about this enigmatic man, however, was defi-
nitely appealing.

Still quite vividly, she recalled the frisson which had
coursed through her each time Lord Merritt had touched
her. Was she prepared, she wondered, to feel those sensations once again?

But the smile his lordship gave her was nothing but
polite. What could she do but accept? Rosamunde slowly
tucked her hand into the crook of Lord Merritt's elbow.

"Remember now, I'm watching you," Peg warned. "And
there's none can pull the wool over the eyes of an old pirate
such as myself!"

Lord Merritt laughed at Peg's jovial warning. He watched
as Rosamunde shook her head at her aged uncle. The breeze
caught deep chestnut wisps and brushed them gently against
her fair cheeks.

"I am quite at a loss," Lord Merritt said, surveying the
garden which stretched before them. "Which path do you
suggest we take?"

She smiled at him, yet appeared to do so quite cautiously.
What had he done, he wondered, to make her afraid of him?

"Everyone knows, in gardens, as in life, one must always
take the right path," Rosamunde replied, guiding him in
that direction.

"Quite so," Lord Merritt agreed, smiling broadly to allay any of her fears. "Else one will be wrong."

"And left . . . behind," she added, returning his smile.

Poor Roger, Lord Merritt thought, to have merely had Mr. Wickes and his discussions of manure for company on his tour of the garden, while *he* had the good fortune to have the daughter for a guide.

" 'Twould be a pity to leave you, Miss Wickes," he said.

Rosamunde swallowed hard and directed his attention to the nearest rosebush. She knew quite a bit about the garden—and, thankfully, not a word was said of rainfall or manure!

At the far end of the garden, Rosamunde stopped. Lord Merritt felt a great deal of regret when she slowly released his arm.

In spite of the pleasant discussion they had been having as they strolled through the garden, her gray-blue eyes were exceptionally serious—he might almost have said troubled—when she looked into his.

Lord Merritt was seized with the urge to enfold her in his arms until the worry left her lovely eyes. What would Miss Wickes do if he embraced her tiny figure, if he took her chin in his hand and gently lifted her face to his? What would she do if he kissed her?

'Merritt, you're insane!' he scolded himself. He pulled his tall form more erect, the better to distance himself from her. 'You are here for one purpose, and one purpose alone—to determine what, if anything, Dudley Wickes knows of the Penderrick fortune, and, if possible, to reclaim it. You most certainly cannot involve yourself with the niece of the man you suspect of stealing it!'

"My lord," Rosamunde said, "I wish to thank you."

Lord Merritt was surprised at this sudden and quite unexpected show of appreciation, especially considering the actions he had just been considering!

"What . . . what have I done to warrant such gratitude, Miss Wickes?" he asked.

"My uncle is old and tired," she began to explain. "He is not well."

"I can see that."

She lowered her gaze. Her long dark lashes overshadowed the gray-blue eyes. Her slender fingers fidgeted with the narrow lace encircling the cuff of her gown.

"After years of being free to sail the seas, sometimes Uncle Peg is very unhappy confined here at Eglantine Cottage," she continued with a sigh. "I do what little I can to cheer him. My father is too busy with his own interests to pay his brother much mind. Mary Ann is too timid to endure his company for long. And Stepmama . . . well, quite plainly, she does not like Uncle Peg."

Lord Merritt nodded. "I rather surmised that, too."

She raised her face to his and smiled shyly into his eyes. "Your interest in his pirate tales has made him happy."

'Blast! Why did she have to say that?' Lord Merritt lamented. He was feeling enough of the pangs of guilt for being interested in the jolly old fellow merely for his purported knowledge of the Penderrick fortune. *Now*, she had to be telling him that he had made Peg happy in the process!

Lord Merritt made what he felt was a safe commentary. "Well, your uncle is a highly imaginative old storyteller."

Her fine brows rose, and she gazed at him with a quite serious expression upon her face. "My uncle is no liar, my lord."

"No, no!" he quickly corrected. "I never meant to imply . . ."

"Of course you did not," she said.

Lord Merritt eyed her cautiously. "You cannot mean to say that your uncle's stories are all true."

"You must understand about pirate tales," she said as she resumed her stroll down the brick path. His lordship walked beside her. "Imagine months confined aboard ship, with little else to do but recount stories, stories which one has heard repeatedly over the years, stories which are told and retold long after their original tellers have died."

"Such as the tale of Port Royal?"

She nodded. "And while no pirate can resist making a good tale just a little better . . ."

"There is truth behind each tale?" Lord Merritt finished for her.

Even though she made no reply, Rosamunde raised one fine eyebrow and shrugged.

Lord Merritt watched her, uncertain of what to say. He held himself as rigid as possible in order to hide the surge of excitement which shivered in the muscles of his arms. Peg was not mad, nor a liar. And if his tales held but a grain of sense and truth, perhaps there was yet hope of regaining the lost Penderrick fortune.

——EIGHT——

Lord Merritt rubbed his smoothly shaven chin and nodded. Fickle had managed to shave him without slitting his throat. His mother had not yet poisoned them. His cousin had not stolen his horses—yet.

As he left the master bedchamber, Lord Merritt noted that Fickle's aunt and the housemaid had brought the place just barely up to his own rigid specifications.

Lord Merritt nodded with satisfaction as he descended the staircase.

"Duck!"

He barely dodged the flying cricket ball. It careened off the wall and bounced down the stairs, to be quickly retrieved by the youngest Fickle sibling. The rest of the players scattered into the dark recesses of unoccupied rooms.

Lord Merritt descended the rest of the stairs, then stood there, pointing straight down in front of him. Terrence slowly approached, scuffling his shoes as he came.

His lordship held out his hand. Reluctantly, Terrence relinquished the ball.

"I thought you were told not to do this again," Lord Merritt said, frowning at the boy.

"I was told to keep the ball out of your applesauce," Terrence corrected.

Lord Merritt pursed his lips and studied the ball as he turned it round and round in his long fingers until he had

completely subdued the laughter which threatened to burst
forth.

"I see I shall have to be more specific. Either the ball
stays or you stay at Penderrick Keep. The choice is yours."

Terrence's two small ears grew red. He stared at the floor
and jabbed his toe at the point where two pieces of parquet
met. "Yes, m'lord," he mumbled.

Lord Merritt tossed the ball into the grubby, outstretched
hands. He waited until Terrence was well out of range
before allowing himself to chuckle softly.

He shook his head. Perhaps it had something to do with
Mrs. Fickle's way with a meal. Perhaps he was becoming
more mellow with age. *Never* had he imagined he could
have tolerated children in his household.

Fickle waylaid him on his way to his customary breakfast
place in the drawing room. "A caller, m'lord."

"Has this to do with estate business?" his lordship asked,
a puzzled frown creasing his brow.

"The caller wasn't too informative, m'lord, but I think
not."

Lord Merritt turned toward the drawing room. "Show
him in."

He could only hope this caller was more informative than
Raikes and Gidley. He certainly could not be more bothersome.

The stout man stood in the doorway, his limp felt hat
clutched in his hammy fists. He passed his large hand across
his brow and over his bald head.

"Your lordship," the man said. He dipped the upper part
of his stocky body in a short, quick bow. Then he proceeded
into the room, making directly for his lordship.

Lord Merritt continued to study his caller. There was
something about him which led him to believe that the man
was not of the same caliber as the crafty Raikes or the
skulking Gidley. Still, he felt compelled to exercise extreme
caution as well in his dealings with this unknown man.

"I've not had the pleasure, sir," Lord Merritt replied.

"John Childers, m'lord, at your service," the man replied, bowing again.

Lord Merritt studied this John Childers. He did not have the look of a gentleman, yet he was not in service, else he would have pulled a forelock instead of executing a bow.

"And the reason for your call?" Lord Merritt asked. He gestured to a chair, then seated himself in the one opposite.

"I've recently returned to these parts," Mr. Childers explained as he eased his broad frame into the delicate chair.

"From the war?"

"Indeed, I was in service to the Crown," he answered slowly. "You have purchased the Keep, m'lord?"

"It is an inheritance."

"Oh," Mr. Childers said. "I am sorry to hear Sir Harold died."

A look not of sorrow, but more of what Lord Merritt would have termed disappointment flickered briefly across the man's eyes.

"You were acquainted with my grandfather?" Lord Merritt asked.

"Only in passing," he answered. After a pause, he asked, "Since Sir Harold is now dead, might I presume upon your lordship to assist me?"

'Ah, so there *is* a reason for this call beyond merely offering his condolences,' Lord Merritt thought, gratified to find that his suspicions of the man were not totally unfounded.

"How so?" his lordship asked cautiously.

"I was hoping perhaps to renew an old acquaintance with one whom, unfortunately, I have lost contact over the years. A Mr. Raikes," Mr. Childers offered, then paused.

Lord Merritt made no response, yet all the while he was busily assessing the man who stood before him. He had a right to be doubly cautious of Mr. Childers. Could anyone who had been an associate of the dubious Raikes be trusted completely? Well, perhaps Peg—but then again, Lord

Merritt thought with a small chuckle, he was not so certain he could completely trust that crusty old prevaricator, either.

"I have heard that Mr. Raikes has called here, m'lord."

"Briefly," Lord Merritt replied. How the deuce did this man know of the comings and goings of persons at Penderrick Keep? His lordship most assuredly did not like this turn in the matter.

"Would you perhaps know where Mr. Raikes is staying?"

Lord Merritt frowned. If Childers already knew so much about Raikes' activities regarding himself and Penderrick Keep, surely he would know where Raikes was staying. On the other hand, Raikes was a secretive fellow. Yet, why would he need to hide from an associate with friendly intentions?

"I am merely visiting this area, Mr. Childers. If it is information you seek, perhaps you should make inquiries at the local inn," his lordship suggested, reluctant at this point to disclose freely any information.

"Ah, that would be the Dead Man's Head Inn. Yes, I'm acquainted with that establishment," Childers said, nodding. "Thank you for your cooperation, m'lord."

The man rose to leave, then suddenly paused and turned. "By the bye, m'lord, the last I was in these parts there was a charming family living at Eglantine Cottage, the Wickes. Would you have met them yet?"

"You appear to be familiar with my callers, Mr. Childers. Do you not also know upon whom I have called?" Lord Merritt asked sarcastically.

"Oh, m'lord, I wouldn't presume," Mr. Childers humbly declared. "I was merely curious as to whether you had had the opportunity to converse with the old man, Dudley Wickes—Peg, I believe some call him."

Lord Merritt frowned. First this strange man made inquiries regarding Raikes. Now Mr. Childers was pursuing the Wickes. Lord Merritt was not about to allow this

stranger access to the ill and aged man, nor to the rest of the
defenseless Wickes family!

"Mr. Childers, unlike yourself, I am not in the habit of
following the movements of my neighbors," Lord Merritt
said coldly. "If it is information you seek regarding any of
the persons in the area, perhaps you should contact the
Ladies' Society for the Charitable Assistance of the Worthy
Poor. I understand those good beldames are a veritable
treasure trove of information regarding persons of their
acquaintance. " Lord Merritt grinned and added, "And even
more information regarding persons whose acquaintance
they have not made."

Mr. Childers' lips twisted into a wry smile. "Perhaps I
shall do just that, m'lord."

Lord Merritt frowned as he watched the man leave. With
each passing day, the situation here was becoming increasingly bizarre.

Rosamunde opened the door to Lord Merritt. At the very
sight of him, her heart thumped against her breast as if
knocking to be let out.

How utterly ridiculous to feel this way, she chided
herself. 'The man has come to visit your uncle, not you,
you silly goose. How could you possibly believe his
lordship would be interested in poor, plain, insignificant
little you?'

Yet he was gazing down upon her with more than mere
social politeness. Oh, did his eyes *have* to be so blue?

"Good day, Miss Wickes," he said, smiling.

She gathered enough of her wits about her to say, "Do
come in, my lord. I . . . I thought perhaps you had
decided not to call again."

"I have missed visiting you . . . and your family,"
Lord Merritt replied as he entered the hall. "I have been
impatiently awaiting a most important delivery. Is your
uncle receiving today?"

"I believe he would always receive you, my lord. He has

spent the past few days debating which tale to tell you next," she replied with a laugh.

The Rosamunde noticed the huge, lumbering wagon which sat before their home. "My lord, did some mishap befall your horse and your carriage?"

"Have you not heard?" his lordship asked with feigned surprise. "A wagon is the current rage in London as a gentleman's transportation."

Rosamunde eyed the wagon again, then turned a mischievous smile to Lord Merritt. "Indeed, such an enormous rig must make you a veritable Corinthian."

His lordship merely smiled at her enigmatically and proceeded into the sitting room.

Peg was seated in his customary chair. He peered with keen interest out the window.

"In the hope that you will forgive my lapse in visiting you, Peg, I have brought a peace offering." Lord Merritt said.

"Do ye think it will take us as long to arrange a peace as they took in Vienna that ye need bring it in a wagon?" Peg asked, gesturing toward the view through the open window.

Lord Merritt turned, anxiously watching the doorway. Two young men had lifted their burden from the back of the wagon.

"I know it is not a redhead from Cherbourg," his lordship began his apology. "However, I think this might assist you in getting about a bit better than she." Lord Merritt stepped to the side as two young men wheeled a Bath chair into Eglantine Cottage.

"Oh, Lord Merritt!" Rosamunde managed to gasp in surprise.

Peg sat there quite speechless.

"How kind of you, my lord!" Mrs. Wickes exclaimed, bustling up to the Bath chair and then to Lord Merritt. "Is this not too, too kind of his lordship, Mary Ann?"

Mary Ann nodded.

"Why, he must think a great deal of you—and the family—to bestow such a thoughtful, and useful, gift."

Rosamunde decided to throttle Stepmama at the earliest opportunity.

"This is much more appropriate than that wretched peg," Mrs. Wickes continued. "Especially for a gentleman of your years, Dudley." She ran her hand over the smoothly turned wooden wheels. "And how much better this will be for the carpet as well."

"I cannot accept this," Peg finally grumbled.

"Whyever not!" Mrs. Wickes demanded. "How can you insult his lordship in this way?"

"It *is* very kind, Uncle Peg," Rosamunde added.

"I cannot accept this," Peg insisted. "I have never taken charity."

"Charity!" Lord Merritt exclaimed.

"Oh, now you've done it, Dudley," Mrs. Wickes scolded. "Gone and angered his lordship."

"This is not charity," Lord Merritt said. "This is a gift, from one friend to another!"

"A gift? From a friend?" Peg repeated. "Well, m'lord, since ye put it that way, how can I refuse? I thank ye most heartily."

"If it be your pleasure, sir?" Lord Merritt said, extending his hand in polite invitation to Peg.

Rosamunde watched as his lordship assisted her elderly uncle into his new chair. How kind he was, she thought. How gentle for a man of his size and obvious strength. How manly that he dared show the more tender side of his nature to those less fortunate.

Sir Polly took off from the stationary chair and perched upon the back of the new Bath chair.

"Ah, ye're in for a rare treat, me bucko!" Peg declared to his companion.

Laughing, Peg grasped both wheels and pushed and pulled himself forward and back, as all the while Sir Polly flapped his wings and squawked his approval. Peg experi-

mented with turning his Bath chair first one way, then the
other, until he had succeeded in knocking over a small side
table.

"That is enough, Dudley!" Mrs. Wickes declared. "It
was bad enough when your peg was tearing the carpet. I'll
not have you damaging the furniture as well."

Peg just laughed and spun away from her. Sir Polly
squawked in protest and flapped his wings, the better to stay
on.

Rosamunde turned to watch the author of her uncle's
happiness. Lord Merritt's wide smile made deep vertical
creases in his lean cheeks at the corners of his mouth and
tiny little lines at the corners of his eyes. His silvery-blue
eyes shone with his own apparent delight at having been
able to make Peg happy.

How wrong her first impression of his lordship had been,
Rosamunde decided. He was not the cold, uncaring person
she had supposed him to be. He was reserved, it was true,
one might even say shy. With each visit to Uncle Peg, she
had seen a warmer side of him emerge from the shell in
which he had encased himself. She decided that she liked
this warmer side of his lordship very much. She could not
help but wonder what had happened to cause Lord Merritt to
withdraw into that shell.

"I feel as if I were six years old again!" Peg declared with
glee.

"You *act* as if you were six!" Mrs. Wickes said scornfully.

Peg gave a wicked chuckle and pushed his chair quite
rapidly toward Mrs. Wickes.

"Give us a buss, ye buxom trollop," Sir Polly demanded.

Mrs. Wickes squealed in fright and bustled out of his
way.

"Dudley, this is the outside of enough!" she declared
from her sanctuary behind the sofa. "And that is precisely
where you and that *thing* belong."

"Batten the hatches! We're in for a gale!" Sir Polly warned.

"Catherine," Peg protested, "if ye continue to go on so, ye'll have Lord Merritt believing ye do not appreciate his generous gift."

"I do, I do!" she answered quickly. "I should simply appreciate it more if you were outside."

"Come, Uncle Peg," Rosamunde suggested, "let us see how well this gets you about in the garden."

Rosamunde took hold of the wooden bar across the back of the chair and gave a push. The chair creaked but made no forward motion.

"Hoist anchor!" Sir Polly commanded. "Full sails to the wind, me hearties!"

Rosamunde frowned. She bent over and whispered, "Give us a hand here, Uncle Peg. Pull on the wheels to get this contraption started."

"Allow me, Miss Wickes," Lord Merritt said, stepping to her side. He slid his large, warm hands over hers.

Reluctantly, she slipped out from under his grasp and pulled her hands together. Was she trying to protect them from further contact with his lordship, or was she trying to hold onto the burning sensation which his warm palms had left?

Quite easily, his lordship propelled Peg and the Bath chair across the sitting room and out the wide doors to the stone terrace.

"Come, Rosamunde!" Peg called to her, as enthusiastic as a child with a new toy. "See how it goes!"

She released her own grasp on her hands. Drawing a deep breath, she followed them out to the terrace.

"Don't dawdle, lass," Peg called to her over his shoulder.

She watched in awe as Lord Merritt managed to maneuver Peg and the heavy chair down the three small steps to the brick walk.

"Perhaps if, instead of steps, we have an inclining ramp

constructed there—" Lord Merritt began discussing his plans with Peg.

"While you're about it, see what we can do to smooth this walk!" Peg declared in a voice which shook from the vibrations of the wooden wheels against the unevenly set bricks. "I never realized this walk was so bumpy!"

Peg was immensely pleased with his newly restored mobility. Rosamunde was so happy for him that she, too, smiled.

A faint smile played about Lord Merritt's fine lips as he watched Peg. At times, it appeared to Rosamunde that the man wanted to laugh right out loud, yet somehow always prevented himself from doing so.

She had seen him laugh before. Why did he feel he must continue to hold himself so rigidly in check? she wondered. Strolling beside him now, remembering the touch of him, she could still feel the intense power underlying the surface, and the immense tension that must be necessary to keep such power under his customarily strict control.

She studied his firm profile and his rigid posture. She smoothed one hand over the other as she recalled his warm touch. She suppressed a deep breath as she recalled the sensation of his hand against her breast.

What would happen, do you suppose, Rosamunde speculated, if his lordship should ever decide to unleash such strength? In spite of the warmth of the day, Rosamunde shivered at the unknown and nevertheless highly anticipated consequences of such a prospect.

"'Tis a splendid gift, m'lord," Peg declared as they reached the far end of the garden. "How gratifying to know that, once again, I can escape Catherine whenever I feel the need—which I frequently do, I assure ye."

Rosamunde chuckled. She watched Lord Merritt's fine lips turn up into a grin. She waited for him to laugh. Oh, when would he allow himself to be at ease?

"If it please yer lordship, I believe me old brains have not quite settled yet from the shaking they received on the trip down here," Peg explained as Lord Merritt turned him about to face the sea. "I think I should like to remain here in the sun and the fresh breeze, quite stationary, for just a bit longer."

Lord Merritt nodded. "Then I hope you enjoy the day, Peg. Miss Wickes, please excuse me now."

"Oh, must you leave?" Rosamunde asked quickly. Realizing that she had perhaps made her disappointment a great deal too evident, more slowly, she added, "We . . . my uncle seems to find it so pleasant talking with you."

Lord Merritt looked intently into Rosamunde's eyes. "And I enjoy visiting with you . . . all," he replied, nodding at Peg. "However, Penderrick Keep is greatly in need of my attentions, too. After all, that is why I originally came here."

"I . . . we hope you might call again some time, my lord, if quite convenient," Rosamunde dared to say as she accompanied him up the walk and into the house.

As she escorted him to the front door, Lord Merritt assured her, "I should not miss the opportunity. I should very much like to continue to call upon your family . . . and you, Miss Wickes."

It was almost palpable, the sensation Rosamunde felt emanating from his lordship as she stood before him. He wanted to touch her again. She knew it as she looked into his eyes! And she knew she also wanted to feel once again the touch of his strong hand upon her shoulder or her hands or—She stopped herself. How dare she think such lascivious thoughts!

Even more tangible was the intense reserve by which his lordship managed to keep himself under polite control, and Rosamunde's disappointment as she watched him turn away.

Suddenly Rosamunde smiled to herself, as much in actual pleasure as in surprise. She had known from the beginning that Lord Merritt called for her uncle's company. When had his lordship decided that he also enjoyed hers?

But how could he? she countered herself. He was a viscount, for goodness' sake. She was merely an impoverished spinster. Still, she reflected upon some of her uncle's outlandish tales, stranger things had happened.

She closed the door and passed through the sitting room on her way back to Peg.

Perhaps there was no specific moment which his lordship could pinpoint, she pondered. Perhaps he had come to a gradual realization, just as she herself had realized that Lord Merritt was not only physically attractive, but kind and caring, and possessed of a witty and lighthearted sense of humor. She eagerly anticipated his lordship's next visit.

With a quick, light tread, Rosamunde crossed the terrace and descended the steps. She proceeded down the path until she spied her uncle, seated at the far end of the garden where she and Lord Merritt had left him. Curiously enough, his back was now turned toward the sea.

Her uncle was not alone, either. Those very men who had called previously stood before him again, frowning down upon him in a manner which sent a shiver of fear up Rosamunde's back.

Should she turn quickly and attempt to call for assistance to his lordship and the two husky footmen who had accompanied him? No, Lord Merritt had surely left by now. What could she do?

Protected by the thick vines which grew about the arbor, Rosamunde cautiously approached.

"Ye be a traitor to honest pirates everywhere!" she overheard Raikes' angry accusation.

"I've broken no confidence," Peg replied defensively.

"Ye've taken the treasure and bought yerself that fancy new chair."

"I did no such thing," Peg insisted. " 'Twas a gift from Lord Merritt."

"So much the worse!" Raikes declared. "To tell a landlubber where the treasure be and not yer very own mates."

The more Peg denied their accusations, the more Raikes persisted. All the while, the threatening Gidley towered over her uncle, seated so small and frail in his Bath chair.

Peg's face grew increasingly gray. His frown seemed less from anger than from pain. He drew his limp arm closer to his body. His breathing became more labored. Rosamunde could see the large beads of perspiration dotting his forehead and upper lip.

Her father's spade leaned against the latticework. Seizing it with both hands, she broke into the small clearing beside the arbor.

"Begone with you!" she cried. Shovel blade pointing at the intruders, she advanced upon them. "Can you not see he is ill? Leave now, or I shall summon the constable."

Sir Polly began to squawk and beat his multicolored wings in the air.

Raikes' lips spread in an imitation of a smile, exposing all his rotting teeth. "No need to fuss, me pretty little spitfire," he said. "Our visit is at an end." He bowed to her, then turned and left. The enormous Gidley followed silently behind.

"Rosamunde, my room," Peg whispered weakly.

═NINE═

How he hated to leave, Lord Merritt thought, riding in the lumbering wagon as they returned to Penderrick Keep. He had derived a great deal of pleasure from watching Peg enjoy his gift. He wished he could share Peg's happiness. He had known little of joy with his beleaguered mother. He had learned even less with his harsh father. What little childhood pleasure he had felt, he had quickly learned to suppress. Even more so, he wished he could tell Rosamunde of the happiness that watching her delight had brought him.

Oh, he would call her Miss Wickes to her face. He dare not do less. But in his thoughts, he must refer to her by the more intimate name, for that, indeed, was the nature of his thoughts of her.

And not as a mere dalliance, as Roger had laughingly suggested. Lord Merritt felt he wanted more from Rosamunde. Yet, the situation being as it was, he could not now, in good conscience, ask more from the lady. First he must settle an old score—*after* he had determined if there was, indeed, anything to settle.

He still was not convinced that Peg knew anything of stolen treasure beyond the fantastic tales he had heard recounted—and had himself no doubt perpetuated—countless times over. If there was no treasure, then Lord Merritt might feel free to make his sentiments known to the lady.

And if there was a treasure to be recovered, if her uncle had indeed stolen it—how, then, could he approach her?

He grimaced. He had come to Penzance to claim an unwanted inheritance. How could he have known he would find himself embroiled with aging pirates and stolen treasure—and thoughts of a quite extraordinary lady as well?

Roger was sprawled lazily in the well-worn chair in the drawing room. "An afternoon well spent, no doubt," he commented to Lord Merritt as he entered. "How did Peg like your gift?"

Lord Merritt grinned. "He found it a very moving experience."

"A jest!" Roger exclaimed, shooting upright in his chair. "From the perpetually somber Lawrence Edmonds, Viscount Merritt? Surely I am dreaming!"

Lord Merritt shot his friend a look of playful reproach.

"Aha!" Roger cried, peering intently at Lord Merritt in the gathering darkness. "Very well spent, no doubt. I can see by the look in your eyes. Small wonder you have taken to making frivolous jests."

"I have not the slightest idea what you mean," Lord Merritt stated. He blinked deliberately, then turned from his friend so that he should not so easily give away any other feelings.

"I simply find it rather gratifying to be . . ." His lordship paused, searching for the appropriate word. "Benevolent," he concluded, seating himself in the equally well-worn chair across from Roger.

"Oh, indeed," Roger concurred. "Benevolence was your sole reason for going to all the trouble and expense of obtaining that Bath chair."

"The trouble and expense were insignificant," his lordship said, waving his hand through the air.

"Did your investment pay off? Did Peg at last confide in

you?" Roger asked. He rubbed his hands together with great enthusiasm. "When do we go treasure hunting?"

Lord Merritt shook his head.

"What a pity!" Roger exclaimed with mock dismay. "Now you must return once again to that horrid place filled with all those horrid people, especially the elder daughter."

Lord Merritt twisted his lips to keep from grinning.

"If ye do, ye'd best go quickly," the rasping voice came from out of the twilight.

Roger started in his chair. Lord Merritt rose quickly, every muscle tense with anger.

"I told you once," Lord Merritt said in terse syllables through tightly clenched teeth, "I did not want to see either of you again until such time as *I* summoned you."

His lordship glared disdainfully at the filthy giant and the other distasteful little fellow. While he needed him for his information on Peg and the treasure, his hatred of Raikes was too intense for words.

"Time waits for no man to summon it, m'lord," Raikes said. "Peg is dying."

Lord Merritt caught his breath in apprehension. How could this be? The old fellow was ill, no doubt, but he had seemed so joyously alive barely an hour ago. The cold fingers of sorrow, intertwined with disbelief, gripped at Lord Merritt's heart.

"There be no time left, m'lord."

While this might indeed be his last opportunity to find the lost fortune, Lord Merritt could not, in all good conscience, interrogate Peg and cause the man any additional anguish in his final days—or, perhaps even hours. He shook his head.

"We had a deal, m'lord," Raikes reminded him.

"There is no deal," Lord Merritt answered sharply. "There is no treasure. Peg merely retells the tales he has heard a thousand times. You are insane if you believe him. You are even more insane if you believe that I would badger a dying man for mere fairy tales!"

"There be treasure, indeed, for I have seen it," Raikes

insisted. "If ye cannot be a man of honor and uphold yer end o' the bargain, then I'll be doing it meself!"

"If you harm any of the Wickes, I shall kill you myself, Raikes. I swear it."

"Many have tried, m'lord," he replied. He bowed, then turned on the heel of his well-worn boot. Gidley followed him from the room.

Lord Merritt stood watching the empty doorway. Then at last, he, too, strode toward the door.

"Where are you going, Merritt?" Roger called.

"I'm returning to Eglantine Cottage," he replied. "My friend is dying."

Lord Merritt ignored the fuss Mrs. Wickes made over him when he appeared at their door. He quickly and quietly made his way through the house until he stood at the entrance to Peg's bedchamber.

Silently he watched the scene within.

Rosamunde sat in a little chair at the side of Peg's bed. She tried to spoon warm broth from the small white bowl into his mouth. He turned his head away and sighed.

"You *must* eat, Uncle Peg," she gently insisted.

"I'm tired, Rosamunde," he said. There were no throaty accents nor rasping pirate talk, just a weary, gentle voice.

"Eat to regain your strength," she suggested. "Then you may rest."

Peg nodded toward his left side, completely immobile in the bed. "There is no strength left, my dear."

He sighed again and turned to stare at the fluttering green leaves and the small patch of blue sky visible through the window.

"Twice you have forced me to come to you, Peg," Lord Merritt scolded softly as he appeared at the doorway. "I vow, if news of this is bruited about, you shall surely ruin my reputation." He made his way across the room to stand beside Rosamunde, still seated in her chair.

"Oh, my lord," she whispered, preparing to rise.

Lord Merritt laid his hand gently upon her shoulder, intending more to comfort her than to prevent her from standing.

How small she felt under his hand, how much in need of his support and protection.

How frail Peg looked in the large old bed. If only there were something he could do! Lord Merritt chafed at his own helplessness.

Peg slowly turned his head to face him. A weak smile curved his cracked lips, but Lord Merritt could see that his eyes were tired and lusterless. His lordship suppressed an anguished sigh. Raikes was indeed correct.

"Is she treating you well, old fellow?" Lord Merritt asked Peg, nodding in Rosamunde's direction.

"Well enough," was all Peg answered.

"Do not make her work too hard," Lord Merritt cautioned. "Try to eat what she brings you, so she will not have to carry it all back to the kitchen."

Peg gave him another weak smile. "I shall try, my lord."

Rosamunde took this opportunity to feed several spoonfuls of broth to Peg. Lord Merritt was gratified to see Peg indeed attempt to eat, although in his heart he feared the attempt to be futile.

He waited with the others in the sitting room until it grew quite late. Mary Ann and Mr. Wickes had retired hours ago. Mr. Shelby, who had barely left Mary Ann's side all evening, sat dozing at the other end of the sofa. Eventually even Mrs. Wickes' head dropped back upon the chair and she began to snore loudly.

Lord Merritt quietly rose and made his way to Peg's bedchamber, where Rosamunde alone kept her silent vigil over the sleeping old man.

"How is he?" Lord Merritt whispered.

Rosamunde sighed. "As well as one could expect."

"How are you bearing up, Miss Wickes?" he asked in the same low tones, and yet his voice sounded much softer.

She merely shrugged. Lord Merritt placed his hand on

her shoulder. "You appear very tired. You should be sleeping, too."

She shook her head. "I can't. I must be with him."

Lord Merritt brought in a chair from the dining room and placed it beside her.

"Uncle Peg has been with me for five years, my lord," she said slowly. "He's been more than an uncle. He's been my friend. How can I leave him now?"

Rosamunde looked up at him, her eyes full of question and hurt.

Lord Merritt nodded his understanding. "Then permit me to stay with you, please."

Throughout the night, he stayed with Peg and Rosamunde. There was no need to talk. There was nothing to be said. Lord Merritt merely knew that he wished to be with the old man of whom he had grown so fond. And he wished to be near Rosamunde, to offer her whatever assistance or comfort he could. He sat in the chair close beside her.

As the night wore on, he watched her, suppressing a tender smile at her attempt to remain awake. Drawing in a deep breath, she blinked her eyes rapidly several times and raised her eyebrows as if that would keep her drooping eyelids from closing completely.

"I beg your pardon!" she whispered with alarm when she realized that she had almost fallen asleep in his presence.

Taking care not to make a noise which would disturb the sleeping Peg, Lord Merritt lifted his chair and set it down closer to Rosamunde.

"Come," he whispered, gesturing for her to slip nearer. He placed his arm over the back of her chair and drew her to him.

At first, she resisted. "Oh, no, my lord. 'Tis unseemly."

"What is unseemly," he told her with a gently reproachful smile, "is that I can get no rest watching you for fear you will fall asleep and go tumbling from that chair, waking Peg and doing yourself a damage. How will you care for your uncle if you are injured?"

Too weary to protest further, Rosamunde laid her head upon his shoulder and fell asleep.

He watched her as she slept on his arm. Her thick, dark lashes rested upon her pale cheeks, brushing against the delicate skin. Her breath was sweet and warm as, from time to time, she sighed in her sleep.

Growing weary himself, Lord Merritt rested his head against the top of hers. Her hair was soft against his cheek and smelled of lavender. Such pleasant sensations, he decided. How he would like to repeat the event, many times over—especially under much different circumstances.

The windows of Peg's room were beginning to lighten with the dawn when Peg awoke with a groan. Rosamunde remained at his side while Lord Merritt quietly roused the household.

They all gathered in Peg's bedchamber.

Peg weakly raised his hand to his brother. "Harry, you've been a good brother to me," Peg said. "Even if you did lock me in the cellar whenever our parents went away. I thank you for sharing your home—the upstairs, too—with me these last few years."

With a wry grin upon his face, Peg turned to Mrs. Wickes. "Thank you, too, Catherine."

"Mary Ann," he called to her.

She barely moved from behind Mr. Shelby, where she had taken shelter.

Peg shook his head. "I should like to have known you better, but you were always such a timid little rabbit. What a pity."

Peg looked to the vicar. "Mr. Shelby, I hope you will pray for my forgiveness."

"Indeed I shall," the vicar responded promptly. "I always do."

Much to Lord Merritt's surprise, Peg then turned to him. "I thank you for your friendship in these last few days. I hope you will forgive me, too."

"Forgive you?" Lord Merritt repeated. "There is nothing to forgive, old fellow."

Peg chuckled. Then, in his familiar rasping pirate voice, he began, " 'Twas the early spring o' '76—"

"No, Peg," Lord Merritt protested. "There is no need to tell one of your tales now."

"Indeed there is," Peg insisted. "In 1776, I was a mere lad o' thirteen—they still called me just Dudley then—the second son of an impoverished country squire, with no fortune and no prospects. I took to the sea as a cabin boy aboard the *Halverton*, a merchant vessel out o' Plymouth Harbor. The captain took a liking to me, much to the consternation o' the first mate, one Mr. Raikes, who therefore conceived an immediate dislike o' me."

Rosamunde gasped.

"The threat o' war with the colonials made shipping profits uncertain," Peg continued. "Our captain, not always the most scrupulous o' fellows, decided to turn privateer. It did not seem to matter much to him whether the ship we robbed was French, American, or even English. We came upon the *Dauntless*, heavily laden, returning to Penzance out o' the Carolinas. While I hid quaking with fear under me bunk, they attacked and plundered the ship."

Lord Merritt could not prevent himself from uttering an exclamation of surprise.

"Heading for the safety o' the open sea, and pursued by the vengeful crew o' the *Dauntless*, we were caught in a fierce storm," Peg resumed his tale. "The captain hoped to outrun the gale and reach the safety o' Penzance before we sank. He also hoped that the badly damaged *Dauntless* would sink before it overtook us."

Peg gave a rueful little chuckle. "The Fates would have it otherwise. The captain took the wooden chest containing the Penderrick fortune and forced me into one o' the few cockboats which remained undamaged. At the time, I thought that he was trying to save me life, but he knew that

I hailed from Penzance, and I discovered later that he had other plans for me."

Peg drew in a deep, ragged breath.

"Oh, do rest, Uncle Peg," Rosamunde pleaded. "There is no need—"

"Indeed, my dear, there is," he replied. He swallowed hard and continued. "Me leg was badly injured when the cockboat crashed ashore, but I was alive. The captain forced me to find a hiding place for the chest, intending to wait until a safer time to return and retrieve the fortune. Exhausted, ill, and in great pain from me injuries, I finally collapsed. The captain, his lifeblood draining from him, talking to his pet parrot, was my last memory before I lost consciousness."

Peg's voice was growing increasingly weak. Those assembled drew closer to him, the better to hear his final tale.

"When I regained consciousness, I was in a strange home and lacking a leg. They told me that me leg had been contaminated, and it had to be amputated while I was yet feverish and unconscious. Once they determined who I was, I was sent to my parents' home, this same Eglantine Cottage, to be treated as a bloody invalid—not the life for me," he protested.

"Not you, old fellow," Lord Merritt agreed in a soft, low voice.

"I took to sea again, this time renamed Peg, with Sir Polly—the only other known survivor o' the two wrecks—as my lifelong companion."

Peg turned to Rosemunde and, in a soft voice, asked, "You will care for him now, won't you?"

"Oh, Uncle Peg," Rosamunde said, her eyes brimming with tears. "Need you even ask?"

"Did you later retrieve the treasure?" Mrs. Wickes demanded.

Lord Merritt drew in a deep breath. He had wanted to ask the same question, not from callous greed, but from the curiosity which Peg's tales still had the ability to arouse in him.

"Then I was but a boy, and afraid of the penalties the law would exact from me," Peg answered in a voice that was continually weakening. "After I left, I spent many, many years at sea."

Mrs. Wickes looked about the shabby room. "Could you not have retrieved it these last five years? You can see how much we have needed it."

He chuckled softly. "Anyone could have retrieved it, Catherine, for there was a map."

"A map?" she repeated. Her eyes popped open wide and her jaw dropped. "Where is it?"

"Ah, I warned ye, ye coldhearted bilge rat, that ye'd be sorry ye burnt me leg," Peg revived enough to declare in his best pirate voice. "The map was hidden beneath the padding o' the socket o' me wooden leg."

Mrs. Wickes let out a cry and swooned into Mr. Wickes' arms.

Peg chuckled until he began to cough.

"You all never believed me," he continued in a rapidly faltering voice. "You thought I was just a dotty old man, playing at being a pirate to add a little excitement to my declining years—and to aggravate you, Catherine, which is partially true. But once—and only once—a long, long time ago, I truly was a pirate."

Peg closed his eyes and breathed very slowly. Rosamunde watched him carefully, fearing each breath to be her uncle's last.

Yet Peg opened his eyes once more. Barely able to raise his hand from the bed, he motioned to her. She alone approached his bedside.

"Now that I am dying—"

"Oh, no, Uncle Peg!"

He shook his head to negate her protest. "You are like a daughter to me. I must tell you. . . ."

He reached up and clumsily grabbed her behind the neck, drawing her down to whisper in her ear.

It was not the correct ear. She tried to twist her head so that she could hear whatever it was he wished to tell her upon his deathbed. But his grip was strong, as if he did not want to leave her or this life.

She felt his gasping breath upon her cheek. She knew he was saying something. If only she could know what he had told her!

"Oh, what have I done?" Peg asked, as if suddenly realizing the mistake he had made, yet knowing somehow that there was no more time left in which to correct this error. Then he gave Rosamunde a tiny, reassuring smile. "That's all right, my dear. Sir Polly knows."

Then Peg closed his eyes.

=TEN=

"Such a pity," Miss Sophie pronounced from her place on the threadbare blue damask sofa. As she slowly shook her head, her spectacles slipped farther down her nose.

"Indeed. He was a rather pleasant man," Miss Sarah, seated beside her sister, agreed. Over the top of her spectacles, she peered at the basket of cakes which sat upon the table in front of her, trying to decide which to take next.

"I suppose Dudley had his moments," Mrs. Wickes reluctantly conceded.

Miss Sophie glanced about the small sitting room crowded with mourners. "Many people thought well of him."

Mrs. Wickes nodded a grudging agreement.

"I have not seen so many people at a funeral since . . ." Miss Sophie hesitated. "Well, since . . ."

"Since Nate Boswick died," Miss Sarah supplied for her sister. "Do you not recall? We discovered he had two wives, and everyone came out to see the fight when they both attended the funeral."

"Indeed, Dudley has attracted quite a crowd, too," Miss Sophie agreed, glancing about her.

Mrs. Wickes nodded again. "After all, not everyday does one have the opportunity to see the neighborhood pirate buried."

Rosamunde winced at her stepmother's cynicism. She was seated in Uncle Peg's customary place and did not intend to move. She could not bear to see anyone else use his chair, at least not so soon.

"Mr. Shelby conducted a lovely service," Miss Sophie said.

"Quite moving," Miss Sarah agreed.

"Mr. Shelby has become quite close to . . . the family recently," Mrs. Wickes informed them, looking pointedly at Rosamunde.

Rosamunde merely grimaced and turned away. Someday, she told herself, perhaps the very next time Stepmama mentioned her and Mr. Shelby in the same breath, she truly would strangle the woman. Yet, at this particular time, she felt she had neither the inclination nor the stamina to escalate the friction between herself and Stepmama.

Let Stepmama make a fool of herself in front of all these ladies, who patently knew that it was not she but Mary Ann who was more than willing to assume that honor.

"You were very close to your uncle, were you not?" Mrs. Thwaitesbury asked Rosamunde.

Rosamunde cleared her throat, yet still had difficulty in finding the words to answer. Staring at her pale hands resting in the lap of her black bombazine skirt, she merely nodded.

"It was so difficult for me actually to comprehend that Mr. Camberton had passed away," the Widow Camberton said. "Sometimes we feel as if a loved one is still with us."

Before anyone could reply, an ear-splitting cry emanated from behind the closed door to what had been Peg's bedchamber.

"Avast, ye lily-livered swabs! Blow the hatch o' this brig or I'll give ye a taste o' me broadsword!" The rasping voice carried through the door, down the short hallway, and into the crowded sitting room.

Mrs. Thwaitesbury looked wide-eyed at the Widow Camberton. Miss Sophie slowly edged her spectacles higher up upon her long nose and peered at her sister, who was cautiously looking about over the top of her spectacles. The rest of the mourners, scattered about the sitting room, also paused in their conversations.

"My late brother-in-law's parrot," Mrs. Wickes hastily explained. Mrs. Thwaitesbury turned to the Widow Camberton and sighed with obvious relief.

"I do so wish I could rid myself of that tiresome bird," Mrs. Wickes continued to complain. "Please, pay no heed to whatever he may say. I suppose he, too, has been rather distraught over Dudley's recent demise."

"I suppose so," Mrs. Thwaitesbury agreed.

"My grandfather had a spaniel," the Widow Camberton said. "After my grandfather passed away, that dog never ate a bite, just sat by his grave until he died there."

"Indeed?" Mrs. Wickes looked rather hopeful. "Do you suppose Sir Polly might do the same?"

"Ye'll not be harming Sir Polly!" Rosamunde protested, springing forward in the chair. Shocked at how much she sounded like her uncle, she said more quietly, "Uncle Peg specifically requested that I care for him now that . . . now that he cannot."

"Was that your uncle's dying request to you?" Mrs. Thwaitesbury asked.

Without thinking, Rosamunde shook her head.

"What was, my dear, if I may be so bold as to ask?" the Widow Camberton inquired.

"I . . . I . . ." Rosamunde stammered. How could she respond? How could she tell them what she had not heard?

"Ours was purely a marriage of convenience," the Widow Camberton plunged ahead, not really waiting for Rosamunde's reply. "Yet, when he passed away, Mr. Camberton's last words to me were that he had grown to love me."

"How touching," Mrs. Thwaitesbury declared. Her wrinkled lips twisted into a grimace. "I shall look for no such sentiments from *my* husband."

"Bollixy swab! Keelhaul the bilge rat!" Sir Polly's voice rang through the house in spite of the tightly closed door.

"Oh, do quiet that animal!" Mrs. Wickes ordered Rosamunde.

With immense relief, Rosamunde excused herself. She did not want to appear rude. These were kind friends and neighbors who had come to pay their last respects to Uncle Peg. She merely wished that, at this moment, she could avoid people altogether.

Yet her short journey down the hall to the privacy of Peg's bedchamber was beset with blockades at every turn. Friends and neighbors were continually stopping her to express sympathies which they had expressed several times before.

But Rosamunde did not recognize the man who now approached her. She could not recall ever having seen the stockily built man before. Was he an old friend of Uncle Peg's?

"My condolences, Miss Wickes, to you and your family," he said, running his hand over his smooth bald head.

"Thank you for coming, sir," she replied politely. "I know you are not a neighbor. Were you a friend of my uncle?"

"I was perhaps better acquainted with him than he with me," the man answered.

What an extremely odd thing for a person to say, Rosamunde decided.

"I was greatly distressed that Peg died before I had an opportunity to speak with him," the man said. "Were you with him when he passed away?"

Rosamunde paused, her heart chilling with apprehension. The man had called her uncle Peg. So had that odious Mr. Raikes. Had this man been a pirate, too?

Her initial reaction was to flee as quickly as possible. She glanced about for aid, but her father and stepmother were occupied elsewhere, and she knew as surely as night follows day that no assistance would be forthcoming from

Mary Ann. Best to proceed with caution then, she decided.

"We all were with him," Rosamunde replied. She nodded politely, then continued on her way.

"How comforting," the man offered, following her. "Did he perhaps have some last words to pass on to you all?"

While Uncle Peg had been alive, no one had taken his tales of pirate treasure seriously. Why were so many people, even absolute strangers, now so suddenly interested in what had been his last words?

"I am afraid my uncle was too ill to say much of anything," she replied. "Pray, excuse me."

Although she had already spoken to Mr. Shelby, and could think of very little else to say to the man, she was greatly relieved to see him. Quickly, she made her way toward the Silent Vicar.

"You appear overwrought, Miss Wickes," Mr. Shelby commented. "This is a trying time for all. I do hope you are having a care for your own welfare."

Rosamunde nodded.

"When all have returned to their homes, I hope you will take a quiet moment to reflect upon the fond memories you have of your uncle," he suggested.

Rosamunde nodded again. She never had considered Mr. Shelby so awfully obnoxious. He truly was a very pleasant, considerate man.

"I realize you and your uncle were very close," Mr. Shelby continued. "Perhaps it would provide some comfort to take the time to reflect upon his last words to you."

Rosamunde looked up sharply at him. Oh, no! Not the vicar! How disappointing to think that he, too, was only interested in Uncle Peg's treasure.

"I think not, Mr. Shelby," she replied coolly. "Pray, excuse me." Quickly, she proceeded down the hallway, entered Peg's room, and firmly closed the door behind her.

"Oh, dear," Mr. Shelby lamented aloud, as he stood there, staring after her retreating figure.

As yet, Lord Merritt had only briefly been able to offer

Rosamunde his sympathy. Now was his opportunity to talk with her further. As he approached, he overheard her abruptly terminated conversation with the vicar.

"A problem, sir?" he asked, coming up beside Mr. Shelby.

Mr. Shelby's brows were drawn down into a troubled frown. The corners of his mouth hung low with dejection. Lord Merritt decided that the vicar rather reminded him of a forlorn little hound puppy, except his ears were shorter.

"I have offended her," Mr. Shelby replied.

"How so?"

"I merely attempted to comfort Miss Wickes by reminding her how precious a loved one's last words can be," Mr. Shelby said. "What could she find so offensive in that?"

"Miss Wickes has been exceedingly distraught. I should not be too concerned."

Mr. Shelby gave a sigh of relief, then wandered off in search of more of those little sandwiches.

Lord Merritt stood in a corner from which he could easily view the doorway to Peg's bedchamber, and waited for Rosamunde's reappearance.

"Oh, Lord Merritt! What an honor! What a privilege!" The plump lady in the dark purple gown dipped an extraordinarily deep curtsy in front of him. He noted the plump young girl standing behind her.

"I am not the king, madame," he informed her in his habitually cool manner. "A simple good day will suffice."

Good day and good-bye, his lordship silently concluded. He could detect a matchmaking mama from a mile away, and he wanted no part of this one. Had these people no sensibilities, that they must search for husbands even at a funeral?

Lord Merritt did not dwell upon either of them for too long, though, as he wanted to keep a watchful eye for Rosamunde's return.

"We have been intimate friends of the family for ever so long. Did Dudley never mention Mrs. Morley to you?"

"No, never," Lord Merritt replied.

"Imagine, your being acquainted with Dudley as well, and our having never been introduced before," she continued, apparently undaunted by his lordship's forbidding reserve.

"Imagine."

"Well, I suppose, as we had a mutual acquaintance in poor old Dudley, it is quite fitting that we finally meet."

Rarely had he encountered such persistence, his lordship decided—except perhaps in that dog at the one and only extraordinarily disgusting bullbaiting he had attended. And, now that he gave the matter some thought, the woman did rather resemble that tenacious little dog.

"My daughter, Harriette, makes her come out this spring, although I daresay we might attend the Little Season this autumn," Mrs. Morley continued. "I suppose now that we have been introduced, we shall see you quite frequently in London."

"Oh, I assure you, Mrs. Morley," Lord Merritt said, "I shall be looking for you. Now, pray excuse me."

Before Mrs. Morley could launch into another monologue, Lord Merritt left her, making a tortuous attempt to cross the crowded sitting room.

Rosamunde had at last left Peg's bedchamber. Yet she could not proceed down the hall to enter the sitting room. Raikes and Gidley stood before her, preventing her from moving in any direction.

The unmitigated gall of those men! Lord Merritt seethed with anger as he caught sight of them. When had they entered the cottage? Blast Mrs. Morley, too, for distracting him when he should have been watching out for Rosamunde. And blast himself, too! He should have been paying better attention.

"I know Peg had a last word to ye," Raikes said.

"The final words of affection between a niece and a favored uncle are private, Mr. Raikes," she replied, her chin lifted bravely in the air.

She tried to slide to the side, but Gidley blocked her way. She pressed her back against the door.

Lord Merritt muttered his apologies to each person he pushed aside in his efforts to reach Rosamunde quickly.

"Perhaps ye be such a favored niece that he indicated to ye where his treasure might be hid," Raikes suggested.

Rosamunde gave a little snort of exasperation. She gestured to the peeling paper on the wall and the threadbare carpet which ran down the hallway. "Does it look as if my uncle had a treasure? I saw you speak with him many times and *always* he insisted he had none. Why would you not believe him?"

"Because I *know* he did. And I believe ye, too, now know its location," Raikes said.

Rosamunde said nothing, but defiantly glared at him.

"Peg was a tough, old pirate who would not talk. However," he continued, his beady eyes raking her figure, "ye being a young lady, gently bred, perhaps there be something which Gidley and meself can say, or do, to induce ye to disclose what information Peg passed on to ye with his dying breath."

Gidley took one threatening step closer to her.

Lord Merritt came up behind the two men. Hooking the toe of his boot about Gidley's ankle, he shoved his broad shoulder into the man's back. Gidley slammed sideways into the wall. Quickly, Lord Merritt slipped into the space between Raikes and Rosamunde.

At the sight of his lordship, Raikes took one slow step backward. Gidley, righting himself, glared angrily at his attacker, but, after a sharp look from Raikes, quickly drew back.

A sly grin slowly spread across Raikes' face. "Perhaps I've underestimated ye, m'lord." He bowed to Rosamunde. "Good day, Miss Wickes. Perhaps we'll meet again."

"I highly doubt it, Mr. Raikes," she informed him haughtily.

"Didn't the good reverend teach ye not to doubt?" Raikes

asked with a menacing leer. Then he and Gidley strode down the hall and left the cottage.

Rosamunde wanted to remain strong and in control of her emotions in Lord Merritt's presence. She didn't want this extraordinarily self-possessed man to think her weak and missish. Yet Rosamunde found she needed to rest her back against the wall to keep from collapsing.

"Miss Wickes. Rosamunde," Lord Merritt said softly. He lifted his hand to her shoulder as he moved to stand before her. "Did they harm you?"

He placed his other hand upon her arm. He ran his hands up and down her arms, slowly, as if searching for injuries. She knew Raikes and Gidley had not harmed her—not yet—but the pounding of her own heart at Lord Merritt's gentle touch made her breast ache.

She was relieved to be with him, glad to feel his touch. The encounter with the sinister pair had left her unsettled and bewildered. Lord Merritt's very presence gave her a welcomed sense of security.

"They . . . they want to know where the treasure is. They threatened . . ." She could not explain further. The very thoughts of what those two might resort to in order to obtain the long-sought treasure made her shiver with fear.

"I am so glad you are safe," he said.

"I'm glad you were here . . ."

"I want to keep you safe, Rosamunde."

She looked up into Lord Merritt's blue eyes. They were no longer icily cold. Neither did they give her the impression of being silvered mirrors which only reflected back an image rather than letting one glimpse what lay beneath the surface. Lord Merritt's eyes were warm with concern for her. Their inviting depths drew her in.

As he held her, the blue of his eyes grew increasingly warmer until they turned to white-hot flame. He stepped closer to her.

She felt his breath upon her cheek, warm and sweet.

Slowly, he lowered his face until his lips touched hers, softly, gently.

He drew back after that first tiny kiss. He released her. His eyes still revealed the fire burning within him. Nevertheless, he managed to keep it in check, simmering just below the surface. He removed his hands from her shoulders. His smile held the same sweet sadness which she, too, felt at separating from him.

"Come, Rosamunde," he said. " 'Tis not the appropriate time. Later, we must talk."

Rosamunde offered no resistance as he led her into the sitting room. She settled uneasily into Uncle Peg's chair. With great reluctance, she watched Lord Merritt bid Mr. and Mrs. Wickes good afternoon and then depart.

It took several minutes before Rosamunde could regain her senses and understand what was transpiring about her. She raised her hands to her cheeks. Were they as burning red to other people's observation as they felt to her own touch?

She brushed the palm of her hand against her lips, remembering the feel and even the taste of Lord Merritt's kiss.

He had been such a comfort to her during Uncle Peg's last hours. He was the only one, she felt, who actually cared for her uncle almost as much as she did. He had actually taken the time to listen to the old man. And now she knew he cared for her. He cared not just about her physical well-being, but about her inner feelings as well. He would never be so callous as to pry into those private moments she had shared with her uncle.

She allowed a tiny smile to curl the corners of her lips. Lord Merritt had appeared like a knight-errant to rescue her from the vicious Raikes and that horrid Gidley.

Then her shoulders shivered. Whatever would she do if they returned? *When* they returned, she corrected herself. She had no doubt those two would not let the situation rest.

How would she escape them again without Lord Merritt's assistance?

How had she escaped them this first time? she began to wonder. Upon confronting Lord Merritt, those two villains had certainly retreated quickly—too quickly, she decided with a worried frown.

How could those two ruffians have ever encountered Lord Merritt before? Yet Raikes had called him "m'lord." As a matter of fact, Raikes had said . . . what had he said? She was so upset that everything melded into a blur. Raikes had said something about underestimating his lordship, of that she was certain.

She shook her head to try to clear her thoughts. She had a deep-rooted apprehension that she was going to need all her wits about her to sort this one out.

Raikes had said he had underestimated Lord Merritt. Now, she reasoned, in order to underestimate someone, must not they have met them beforehand in order to make a first estimation that was *under* the estimation which they were making now . . . ? Oh, she was so confused!

There was one thing of which she could be certain. Raikes and Gidley *knew* Lord Merritt—and *he* knew *them*. As a matter of fact, it appeared to her as if Raikes and Gidley were a bit cautious of his lordship. Was Lord Merritt seeking his family's lost treasure with the assistance of those two old pirates?

Rosamunde pressed her lips tightly against each other. Lord Merritt had used Uncle Peg! His interest in the old man's sea tales was merely a ruse to get him to disclose the location of the treasure.

Lord Merritt had taken advantage of her, too—and was still intending to—the callous, coldhearted beast! Was her rescue by his lordship from the threats of Raikes and Gidley even part of his scheme to pretend to be the hero?

Oh, his lordship probably thought he had covered all possibilities. If Raikes and Gidley could not obtain the information from her by threats, then his lordship had plans to obtain it from her by other, more pleasurable means.

If that were the case, Rosamunde thought, her brow creasing with hurt and growing anger, then his lordship was the one who had seriously underestimated this pirate's niece!

For the past three days she had wept tears of sorrow. Now she fought back hot tears of rage. She harshly rubbed the back of her hand against her lips, trying to erase the warmth of the kiss which still burned against them.

"Merritt! Are you sleeping upon that horse?" Roger demanded loudly as they rode back to Penderrick Keep. "I said, what do you intend to do now?"

Lord Merritt, roused from his reverie, looked at his friend with puzzled surprise. How could Roger know that he had plans for Rosamunde? Then he realized, with immeasurable relief, that he and Roger were discussing two entirely different matters.

"So sorry, Roger," Lord Merritt replied. "What were you saying?"

"What will you do now?"

Lord Merritt shrugged. "I . . . I truly am uncertain as to how to proceed."

"There is precious little chance of finding the treasure now that Peg is dead."

Lord Merritt could only allow himself to nod.

"Raikes and Gidley know nothing, else they would not continue to bother you," Roger reasoned.

"That is true," Lord Merritt agreed. He decided against telling Roger that he had added John Childers' name to the list of persons seeking the treasure.

"I have observed that Peg was not that close to any other members of the Wickes family," Roger continued. "And you say that Miss Wickes also knows nothing?"

Of course she knew nothing. Lord Merritt did not even want to suspect that she knew and was withholding the

information. He did not want to question her, to have her
believe that he was merely using her to regain his mother's
family's lost fortune. He would rather lose the fortune than
lose the lady.

"While no one can be certain of Peg's last words to his
niece," Lord Merritt hedged, "I truly do not think the two
were discussing where treasure might be found."

Roger twisted his lips into a wry grin and nodded. "Then
we have made an end of it, Merritt."

"Perhaps not," Lord Merritt replied.

"Who else can we question? All those who might have
witnessed the event are dead."

"Not quite. There is yet one who might be prevailed
upon—"

"Not Raikes, nor Gidley . . . then who?"

"Sir Polly."

Roger burst into laughter. "Now I know you are mad!"

He had heard Peg say quite clearly that Sir Polly knew,
Lord Merritt silently recalled. What else could he be
referring to?

"Sir Polly is a *bird*, Merritt," Roger reminded his friend.
"He only repeats what someone else has taught him."

" 'Tis worth the try," Lord Merritt offered.

Who knew what Sir Polly had been taught to repeat over
the many years he had been the companion of various
sailors—or pirates? Did Peg himself not say that he had
collapsed upon the shore the night of the shipwreck to the
sound of the captain talking to Sir Polly?

'Twould be worth trying to get the bird to talk, especially
if it meant retrieving the lost Penderrick fortune without
encumbering Rosemunde with further worries. Now, if only
he could devise a way to speak with Sir Polly alone . . .

"How will you induce Sir Polly to disclose the location?"
Roger asked, his eyes alight with merriment. "Bribe him
with sunflower seeds? Perhaps a nice, juicy . . . what do
parrots eat, Merritt?"

Lord Merritt ignored his friend's sarcasm. His mind was busily forming a plan.

"I see there is no diverting you, Merritt," Roger conceded. "Well, I suppose 'twill be more pleasant dealing with the parrot than with Raikes and Gidley."

═ELEVEN═

"I thought they would *never* leave! They certainly ate enough," Mrs. Wickes complained. She carefully tallied how many small cakes were left in the basket. "Oh, bother. And I was hoping to have enough left to make a tipsy cake tomorrow."

"They were all very kind to come," Mary Ann commented. "Especially Mr. Shelby."

"Well, 'tis his job," Mr. Wickes grumbled, staring with longing at his neglected garden.

"I'm sure Mr. Shelby was a great comfort to you, my dear," Mrs. Wickes said to Rosamunde.

Obviously, Rosamunde decided, Stepmama was so preoccupied with her grandiose matchmaking schemes that she was completely unaware of what was actually happening at Eglantine Cottage.

"Rarely have I seen people so preoccupied with a dying man's last words," Mr. Wickes commented. "I don't know how many people asked me . . . even people I had never met."

Rosamunde swallowed hard.

Quite unexpectedly, Mrs. Wickes came up beside Rosamunde and placed her arm about her shoulders, causing her to draw back with a start.

The shock of Uncle Peg's dying must surely be the cause, Rosamunde reasoned, for this unaccustomed display of motherly affection from Stepmama.

"How touching that Dudley chose to impart some last words of wisdom to you, my dear," Mrs. Wickes said.

In the five years that he had lived with them, Rosamunde had never heard Stepmama refer to Uncle Peg as wise.

"I am certain that, with his vast experience, Dudley had acquired quite a deeper perspective on life and its meaning," Mrs. Wickes continued. "Why do you not share those lovely last words with us now?"

"I . . . I think not."

"Oh, come now," Mrs. Wickes cajoled. "Surely, you are not still put out with me for burning Dudley's wooden leg, are you?"

Rosamunde shook her head. No sense in remaining angry over an act which did not signify anymore, anyway.

Mrs. Wickes dropped her arm from Rosamunde's shoulder as quickly as she had placed it there. "We are all family. You can share with us."

"No, I cannot, truly . . ."

Mrs. Wickes placed her hands upon her ample hips and glared at Rosamunde. "So this is what it all comes down to, does it not? The plain and simple truth is that I am not your real mother, and you have never considered me as such . . ." Mrs. Wickes pulled her handkerchief from the sleeve of her gown and began to dab at dry eyes. "Even though, Lord knows, I have tried and tried, all these years, to be like a mother to you."

"Oh, do not take on so," Rosamunde pleaded. "I cannot tell you because . . ." Dare she reveal the truth—and subject herself to ridicule? There had to be another way, yet the solution stubbornly eluded her.

"I cannot tell you because . . . because I did not hear him," Rosamunde confessed.

Mrs. Wickes looked up from her handkerchief, frowning. "Well, and whyever not?" she demanded crossly. "You were standing directly beside him."

"I . . . I did not hear him because I . . . because he . . . he was gasping so deeply that I could not discern a word he said," Rosamunde said, grateful for the sudden inspiration.

"Well, there's nothing else to be done, then," Mrs. Wickes pronounced, throwing up her hands in defeat. She settled herself on the sofa and brushed her hands up and down the worn cloth. "After all those years of putting up with his wooden leg and his obnoxious parrot and those lurid tales about pirates, and we never got a thing from him," she lamented. She pressed her lips tightly together. "I ask you. Where's the justice?"

"Oh, merciful heavens! What could that be?" Rosamunde exclaimed the next morning.

Sir Polly's raucous squawks again rose from Uncle Peg's room. What on earth was happening to cause him such alarm?

Rosamunde quickly arose, seized her wrapper, and hurried down the stairs. Suddenly she heard the voice of her stepmother as well.

Oh, no! Stepmama with Sir Polly? The woman had continually threatened to do away with the bird. Had she at last decided to make good her threats?

Rosamunde drew up sharply in the doorway to the bedchamber.

"Nice bird. Good Sir Polly," Mrs. Wickes said. She was trying very hard to approach the bird—and Sir Polly was having none of it!

He beat his wings and clawed the air with one long-taloned foot. With each loud squawk, his razor-like beak clacked open and shut.

All in all, he created quite a forbidding-looking picture. Rather effective, too, Rosamunde decided with a grin, as it certainly kept Stepmama at bay.

"Good morning, Sir Polly," Rosamunde called, entering the bedchamber.

Sir Polly calmed immediately. "Morning, lovely lady," he replied in his scratchy little parrot voice.

"However do you get him to speak to you civilly like that?" Mrs. Wickes asked, clearly bewildered.

"By speaking civilly to him."

"What . . . what else can you make him say?" Mrs. Wickes asked coyly.

"Heave to, ye pox-ridden doxy!" Sir Polly cried.

"No, no. I mean, obviously, Sir Polly can repeat words suitable for polite company," Mrs. Wickes insisted. "I just heard him. What *else* can he say?"

"I thought you did not like Sir Polly," Rosamunde evaded.

"Well, I . . . I think perhaps I was mistaken," Mrs. Wickes answered. "He must be a nice bird. After all, Dudley thought enough of him to ask you to care for him." Mrs. Wickes paused and eyed Rosamunde. "And he thought enough of Sir Polly to tell him the same thing he tried to tell you upon his deathbed."

"Whatever do you mean?" Rosamunde asked apprehensively.

Mrs. Wickes fixed Rosamunde with a beady-eyed stare. "Last night, I suddenly remembered what Dudley said. 'That's all right, my dear. Sir Polly knows,' " she quoted.

Rosamunde tried to feign nonchalance. "Sir Polly knew the affection with which Uncle Peg and I . . ."

Mrs. Wickes released a harsh laugh. "I am so glad now that I did not follow my first impulse to destroy that wretched bird as soon as Dudley died. I thought perhaps that what he had said was merely his last futile attempt to keep me from doing just that. But upon reflection, I now know precisely what he meant. Sir Polly knows the location of the treasure."

Mrs. Wickes beckoned Rosamunde to bring Sir Polly into the sitting room.

Rosamunde, with Sir Polly on her shoulder, followed cautiously. Whatever was Stepmama intending now? Rosamunde decided she would continue to keep an eye on both of them.

Mrs. Wickes patted the back of Uncle Peg's old chair and
looked up at Rosamunde with a forced smile. "I think we
shall keep Sir Polly around for a bit longer," Mrs. Wickes
said. "Perhaps we shall even give Sir Polly a place of honor
in our little sitting room so that we can hear *everything* he
has to say, *every* hour of the day."

As the day wore on, however, Mrs. Wickes became
increasingly disappointed. Sir Polly merely sat on his chair.
He said nothing and merely picked at the seeds and pieces
of fresh fruit which the family used attempting to bribe him.

At last Mrs. Wickes became quite worried. "You don't
suppose he will pine away like the Widow Camberton's
grandfather's stupid spaniel, do you?" she demanded of Mr.
Wickes. "Can you imagine anyone not eating?"

Mr. Wickes boldly assessed his wife's ample figure.
"Indeed, I should never believe you capable of such folly,
my dear."

"Now hear this!" Sir Polly cried.

Everyone suddenly snapped to attention and waited in
hushed anticipation for Sir Polly's next pronouncement.

"All hands confined to quarters!"

"All this time waiting and that is all he says?" Mrs.
Wickes complained. She paused, as if thinking hard. "Still
and all, do you suppose . . . ?"

"A clue?" Mr. Wickes suggested.

"I highly doubt . . ." Rosamunde said, trying to insert
some sense into the conversation.

Mr. and Mrs. Wickes could not be bothered with making
sense.

"If he was confined to quarters . . ." Mr. Wickes
mused.

"His bedchamber!" Mrs. Wickes declared, springing
from her chair.

Rosamunde watched in awe as her family rushed to Peg's
bedchamber. There, they proceeded to dismember the old
bedstead and to disembowel the mattress and the chest of
drawers—all to no avail.

"It *has* to be here somewhere!" Mrs. Wickes insisted,

stamping her foot. She paused, then stamped her foot again.
The floorboards emitted a hollow, clunking sound. Mrs.
Wickes' eyes lit up with eager anticipation and she stamped
once again, just for good measure.

"Oh, no, Catherine," Mr. Wickes said, eyeing her foot
with trepidation. "Surely you cannot mean to . . ."

"Harry," Mrs. Wickes ordered imperiously, "get the fire
iron."

The floor of Peg's bedchamber was soon reduced to a
gaping pile of splinters, and the unfortunate Mr. Wickes to
a gasping, perspiring heap, yet the only treasure found were
several broken buttons and a dirty old groat that long ago
had slipped between the cracks.

Mr. Wickes collapsed beside Mrs. Wickes on the blue
damask sofa.

"If that is where the treasure was hidden," he said,
"Dudley must have spent it all."

"Land ho!" Sir Polly cried. "Mount to the crow's nest,
me bucko!"

"Crow's nest?" Mrs. Wickes frowned. "What is a crow's
nest?"

"How should I know?" Mr. Wickes answered testily.

"Well, it was *your* brother that was the pirate. Why, oh,
why, did we not pay more attention to Dudley's stories?"

"The crow's nest is aloft," Rosamunde told them quietly.
"But I do not think . . ."

"Aloft?" Mr. Wickes repeated. He looked toward the
ceiling. "You mean up?"

"Up, as in . . ." Mr. and Mrs. Wickes turned to each
other and cried, "The attic!"

The scramble for the staircase was a sight to behold,
Rosamunde decided. Never had she seen her stepmother
move quite so rapidly. Never had she viewed her stepmother from that angle. She decided that she would rather
not witness such again too soon. Even Mary Ann joined the
eager parade.

Rosamunde followed at a more sedate pace. By the time

she reached the dim, dusty attic, her father, stepmother, and Mary Ann had already succeeded in tearing apart the contents of several large trunks.

Rosamunde regarded the frantic trio with amazement. "I truly do not think . . ."

"These oddments have been here since even before my grandfather was a boy," Mr. Wickes laughed and called out to them from behind a large armoire.

"Did no one in your family ever throw anything away?" Mrs. Wickes complained.

Mr. Wickes opened the armoire, pushed a few faded gowns about on their pegs, then closed the door again, sending up another cloud of dust to further obscure the dark atmosphere of the attic.

Mary Ann opened a large trunk, emitted an ear-splitting scream, then quickly slammed it closed.

"You have found it!" Mrs. Wickes cried. She pushed over several bulging baskets in her rush to get to her daughter's side. "Well, open the trunk!"

"I think not, Mama."

Mrs. Wickes drew back and frowned furiously at Mary Ann.

"I heard that scream—indeed, Dudley probably heard that scream. It was a treasure scream. Now open that trunk," Mrs. Wickes commanded.

" 'Tis not treasure," Mary Ann whined.

"You perfidious girl!" Mrs. Wickes accused. "You have found the treasure and are saying you have not merely so that you can return later and take it and not share with us!"

Rosamunde gaped with sorrowful disbelief at Stepmama's angry accusation. How important could that blasted treasure be if, in searching for it, it so divided her family? She began to wish she had never heard of the awful thing!

Mary Ann groaned and slowly opened the lid, exposing a dead and rapidly decomposing rat. "Are you quite satisfied?" she demanded, slamming the lid shut.

But Mrs. Wickes was not satisfied. The ransacking of the

attic continued until they were far too tired and hungry to continue.

"Perhaps tomorrow we shall have better luck," Mr. Wickes said as he once again collapsed onto the sofa in the sitting room.

Mrs. Wickes was too weary to reply.

"Heave to! Secure the head!" Sir Polly declared.

"The head?" Mrs. Wickes said with a sigh. "But we have already been upstairs."

Mr. Wickes slowly shook his head. "That is not what he means, my dear."

"How do you know what he means?" Mrs. Wickes snapped. "You did not even know what a crow's nest was."

"I think he is referring to the Jericho."

Mrs. Wickes stared wide-eyed at Mr. Wickes. Then she, too, slowly shook her head.

"No treasure is worth that," they decided unanimously.

The house awoke quietly the next morning, yet Rosamunde worried, nevertheless. To what lunacy would Sir Polly's random words prompt her family today?

"Where is your father?" Mrs. Wickes demanded of Rosamunde.

"I have not seen him all morning," Rosamunde answered.

"I thought I saw him heading toward the garden," Mary Ann offered.

"That blasted garden of his! Here we are, desperately seeking a lost treasure, and *he* must shovel manure."

Mrs. Wickes made her way out to the terrace.

"Oh, merciful heavens!" she cried.

Mr. Wickes had apparently spent the early morning searching for treasure after all. Every bush was carefully uprooted, wrapped in coarse burlap, and set upon the brick walk. Throughout the garden, mounds of dirt indicated Mr. Wickes' futile excavations.

At last, Mr. Wickes' red, perspiring face popped up from

one of the holes, rather like a little hedgehog. He emitted a whoop of exultation.

Rosamunde followed Mrs. Wickes and Mary Ann as they ran down the terrace steps. Dodging the uprooted bushes, she made her way down the path to the excavation which held Mr. Wickes.

"Well, did you find it?" Mrs. Wickes demanded, peering carefully over the edge of the hole.

"The shovel hit something."

"Give me a hand," Mrs. Wickes ordered.

Assisted by Mary Ann, Mrs. Wickes scrambled down into the hole with Mr. Wickes.

After much tugging and grunting, Mr. Wickes shook his head sadly. "A rock," he said flatly.

"All this for a rock!" Mrs. Wickes grumbled as she crawled out of the hole.

Rosamunde looked at her filthy, dirt-smudged family. She looked about the decimated garden. She supposed even the field at Waterloo must have looked no worse than this.

"Of course, if you had actually *found* the treasure, I should have been inordinately pleased," Mrs. Wickes informed Mr. Wickes as he, too, vacated the hole. "However, since you did not, I am ever so vexed. I want this all put back exactly as you had it."

"Yes, dear." Mr. Wickes sighed and leaned wearily against his shovel.

"And don't be tracking dirt upon my carpet when you come in."

Rosamunde could only watch with disgust. How could all three of them be so incredibly stupid? The captain of the *Halverton* could not have had access to Eglantine Cottage without the other occupants being aware of it. Uncle Peg had not moved the treasure there from its original hiding place. She had tried to tell them, but her family would not listen. It was impossible for the treasure to be at Eglantine Cottage.

Sir Polly began screeching now, not in anger or in fright, but simply as an alarm.

"No! I shall never listen to another word that stupid bird says!" Mrs. Wickes declared. "Rosamunde, go quiet that miserable creature before I make a pie of him!"

Exceedingly glad to leave the ludicrous scene in the garden, Rosamunde returned to the house.

She came to an abrupt halt at the doorway. Sir Polly was not alone.

Lord Merritt stood before Sir Polly's customary chair. Rosamunde was shocked. How could a man of his lordship's caliber be so rude as to enter their home unbidden? And what was he doing talking to Sir Polly? The longer Rosamunde stood there listening intently to Lord Merritt's words, the angrier and, yes, the more hurt and disappointed she became.

Although Sir Polly's cries drowned him out, she could still discern a few of his lordship's words. Something about treasure—of that there was little doubt. Why, Lord Merritt was every bit as nefarious as Raikes and Gidley!

"How dare you!" Rosamunde raged as she stormed into the sitting room.

Lord Merritt quickly backed away from Sir Polly.

"I beg your pardon. I rapped incessantly, yet no one answered," he offered. "The door was open, so I took the liberty . . . I cannot guess where your housemaid has gotten to—"

"It does not signify that you enter our home unbidden," Rosamunde said. "How dare you question Sir Polly!"

"I . . . he's a charming bird," his lordship stammered. "I enjoy talking to him."

"And hearing him respond, no doubt. Oh, do not stretch my credulity too far, Lord Merritt," she warned. "You duped my poor old uncle. You tried to take advantage of me, too. And now I see that you are not below trying to use an innocent bird in your ruthless greed to regain your family's fortune! How low can you possibly stoop?"

"Not so low that I would deliberately hurt someone I cared about," Lord Merritt answered quietly.

"Cared about?" she repeated, much louder than his lordship. She even managed to drown out Sir Polly's cries. "I thought you cared about Uncle Peg. I . . . I thought you cared about me, but . . ."

He wanted to explain to her. He wanted to enfold her in his arms and wipe away the tears that gathered in her gray-blue eyes. But before he could utter a single word in his own defense, before he could even approach her, Rosamunde turned and fled through the terrace door.

He could have caught her easily on open terrain, but she was more familiar with the twists and turns of the garden paths than he. As it was, he had difficulty in dodging the displaced bushes strewn along the walks. However, once she reached the open field, he was quickly able to overtake her.

Still at a run, he caught her arm and pulled her to a stop. He spun her about to face him and drew her close against his chest. She pushed away from him, trying to escape his embrace, but he held her fast.

"I want nothing to do with them—those greedy, hard-hearted people!" she cried. She tossed her head back in the direction of Eglantine Cottage.

Ah, so that explained why every chest and cupboard in Eglantine Cottage appeared to have exploded, his lordship realized. Her own family was plaguing her with their search for the treasure. What relief it afforded him to know that Rosamunde's anger was not directed solely at him.

"I want nothing to do with you, either!" she declared, glaring up at him. She gave his chest an extra hard push. "If I had my way, I'd put you in that Bath chair you gave my uncle and push you off a cliff!"

She balled her hands into fists and beat against his chest. Slightly painful, he decided, but still he held her, giving her a chance to vent her pent-up sorrow and anger.

Quite unexpectedly, she struck him directly in the gap

between his upward-curving ribs. His breath left him in a rush. Gasping for air, he still would not let her escape, for fear he should never hold her again.

Gradually, her efforts grew weaker as her crying tired her. Eventually she fell against his chest, still sobbing quietly.

He held her close, cradling her in his arms. He reached one hand up to her head and smoothed the back of her dark hair. She was soft to his touch and sweet to his senses. The effort of crying made her warm in his arms.

How he longed to lift her tear-stained face and kiss her once again. He smiled a rueful smile. If he did that, he had not doubt she would fulfill her threat and send him over that cliff.

Then, above the sound of her quiet weeping, Lord Merritt detected another noise of softly rusting leaves. ''Tis the wind,' he told himself, dismissing it from his mind, until he heard it again.

Quite casually, Lord Merritt glanced to his right, over the cliffs out to sea. Directly ahead, he looked toward the low brick wall which surrounded the garden at the back of Eglantine Cottage. Slowly turning only his head to the left, he surveyed the bracken which lined the road that led from Penderrick Keep past Eglantine Cottage into Penzance.

Since when had bracken sprouted eyes? Lord Merritt pondered. It could only have been since pirates, unused to hiding on land, had taken to spying on the occupants of Eglantine Cottage.

Lord Merritt struggled to keep his anger under his customary, tight control. Foolish to confront Raikes and Gidley now, he decided, when he had no weapons at hand, and when anything he might do would only place Rosamunde and perhaps her family in additional danger. Best to get her back to the house, he decided.

Keeping one arm about her shoulder to support her, he drew her toward the house. Indeed, she must have been exhausted with weeping for she offered no resistance.

As they walked along, Lord Merritt's eyes still warily searched the bracken. Perhaps John Childers had not been a pirate after all, he debated, as it had taken his lordship much longer to spot that man, also hidden among the bushes and watching Raikes and Gidley.

Slowly, Lord Merritt brought Rosamunde to the front door. "Will you be all right?" he asked. With great reluctance, he released his hold of her.

Silently, she nodded.

"Please do not misunderstand me, Miss Wickes," he tried to explain. "I truly meant no harm in talking to Sir Polly."

"I do not think you would hurt Sir Polly," she admitted. Her red-rimmed eyes looked directly into his.

"Nor would I harm you," he said, holding her gaze intently. "Surely you must realize that by now."

Rosamunde shrugged. "I suppose not," she said.

She was no longer crying. She was no longer raging with pent-up anger. Then, she looked at him and stated bluntly, "But I still hate you, Lord Merritt, and what you tried to do."

She turned and slammed the door behind her.

═TWELVE═

Rosamunde had always detested the tedious meetings of the Ladies' Society for the Charitable Assistance of the Worthy Poor. The only good thing about Uncle Peg's passing was that she had been able to excuse herself from attending.

Apparently she had missed nothing, as this week's meeting had been exactly the same as the meeting before, and the meeting before that. Although she had no crystal ball, and would not have known how to use one if she did, Rosamunde was quite certain that next week's meeting would be precisely the same again.

In the orange-red light of the setting sun, Rosamunde kicked at pebbles as she trudged up the shadowed, hedgerow-lined road beside Mary Ann. She did not notice the small, dark carriage until it had pulled up directly beside them.

Raikes jumped out of the open carriage door while Gidley quickly swung down from the box. Raikes seized the screaming Mary Ann, who promptly fainted dead away.

The hulking Gidley made a grab for Rosamunde, but she was much lighter and quicker on her feet, and managed to dodge his grasp. Several times the stumbling giant dove for her, yet still she managed to elude him.

"Damn it, man, can't ye catch one girl?" Raikes demanded as he tried to lift Mary Ann's limp body into the carriage.

Gidley merely shot him an angry look. Raikes let Mary

Ann's limp form slide to the ground. He, too, tried to grab
Rosamunde as she ran about to the other side of the
carriage, but he was too old for speed.

As she ran, she searched for a place in the tall hedgerows
wide enough for her to slip through, yet not so wide as to
allow Gidley to pass, but none could be found. She knew
she must not let them catch her, and while she was
anguished at the thought of leaving the helpless Mary Ann
in their clutches, how could she save her stepsister if both of
them were kidnapped?

Yet her hopes of salvation were diminishing as her legs
tired and she began to gasp for breath. She could not
continue to dodge them much longer.

Suddenly Raikes stopped his pursuit of Rosamunde.
"This one is enough. Help me get her into the carriage," he
called to Gidley.

Gidley grabbed Mary Ann about the waist and tossed her
into the dark interior of the carriage as easily as one would
toss a feather pillow.

"Do not summon the constable," Raikes called a warning
to Rosamunde as he climbed into the carriage and closed the
door. "Especially if ye wish to see yer stepsister alive
again."

Gidley hauled himself up onto the box. Taking up the
reins, he slapped them hard against the horse's rump.

"Rest assured, ye'll see her again, safe and sound,"
Raikes said as the carriage sped away, "—once we've been
delivered the treasure."

Overcome with horror and fatigue, Rosamunde collapsed
to her knees in the middle of the narrow country road.

"What shall I do?" she said softly as she sat there alone
in the gathering dark. "Whatever shall we do?"

Why had they taken Mary Ann, who knew nothing? Why
had they left her when Rosamunde knew with dread
certainty that, in a few short moments more, they could
have captured her, too?

Several horses skidded to a stop beside her, casting up a

cloud of dust. She snatched up her skirts, preparing to flee, when she recognized Lord Merritt.

"Miss Wickes! Rosamunde," his lordship cried, quickly dismounting.

"Have you come to pick up what Raikes and Gidley left behind?" she demanded.

He was suddenly at her side, gathering her up in his arms. "What has happened?"

Strangely, it did not matter that she thought him a perfidious wretch who had only used her and her poor old uncle to achieve his own ends, or even that he might be employing those horrid old pirates. She was relieved to nestle into the protection of his strong embrace.

"Raikes. Gidley," she attempted to make her breathless explanation. "Mary Ann."

"Raikes? Gidley?" Lord Merritt repeated.

"Are you surprised?" Rosamunde asked sarcastically.

"Mary Ann!" Mr. Shelby cried, slipping clumsily from his saddle.

"So 'twas those two in that carriage," Roger said. "And they have Miss Bellows?"

Rosamunde nodded helplessly.

"She is in danger?" Mr. Shelby asked.

"More than we may even suppose," Lord Merritt said quietly.

'And how would you know?' Rosamunde wanted to ask.

But Mr. Shelby declared, "Then we must notify the constable immediately." He scrambled to remount his shabby-looking little mare.

"No!" Rosamunde cried, reaching out to stop him. "They will kill her if we do."

"Why have they taken Mary Ann?" Mr. Shelby asked.

"Raikes and Gidley will exchange her for the treasure." Rosamunde shook her head sadly. "A treasure which does not even exist."

Mr. Shelby's round, puppy-dog face blanched, then turned a livid scarlet. "Then she will surely die."

"We will rescue her," Lord Merritt assured him. Then he turned to Rosamunde, and, laying his hand firmly upon her shoulders, he repeated, "We *will*. Now, however, I think it wisest to take Miss Wickes home."

"I'll not go home," Rosamunde protested.

"We must inform Miss Bellows' parents." Gently, with his arm still about her shoulder, Lord Merritt led Rosamunde to his horse. "Mount up behind me."

She drew back from what she had once assumed to be the security of his embrace, uncertain of whether to obey him or not. If his lordship truly were in league with Raikes and Gidley, might he not be delivering her into their clutches? Could she actually trust him?

She looked into his eyes, trying to determine if they were cold, icy-blue mirrors or the warm blue eyes of the man who truly cared for her. Seeing only the deep concentration of a man bent upon his objective, Rosamunde did not know what to believe. Drawing in a deep breath, she complied.

"Mr. Shelby," his lordship said, "will you be accompanying us?"

"I . . . I . . ." The shy little vicar hesitated. "I am afraid that . . . another matter requires my immediate attention. If you will excuse me . . ."

Blast and damn! Rosamunde fumed with silent disappointment as she watched Mr. Shelby bouncing in the saddle as his mare galloped down the road. One can no longer rely even upon the vicar!

"Rosamunde! How could you allow such a thing to happen?" Mrs. Wickes accused after Rosamunde had breathlessly explained what had transpired.

"Had I but known we were to be waylaid," Rosamunde replied sharply, "I would have carried Papa's old pistol with me."

"Could you not at least have held them off just a little longer . . . ?" Mrs. Wickes continued. Leaning a bit closer to Rosamunde, she whispered confidentially, "At least until Lord Merritt arrived?"

"I had no idea his lordship would be riding by, either," Rosamunde reminded her stepmother. She gave a quick, sideways glance at Lord Merritt. The suspicion still haunted her that his lordship had a very *definite* idea that he would be passing that way.

"Then Lord Merritt could have rescued Mary Ann instead of you," Mrs. Wickes lamented wistfully. "Did you not know that the hero rescuing the heroine from danger is what makes them automatically fall in love? Why, anyone who reads a romance novel could tell you that!"

"I shall be certain to make a notation of that fact the very next romance I read."

Did Stepmama believe she harbored no kindly feelings at all toward her timid stepsister? Rosamunde wondered. All the way home, she had lamented the fact that it was Mary Ann and not she who had been kidnapped. She knew herself to be the stronger of the two. However would poor, fainthearted Mary Ann bear up under this ordeal?

"I should not be too hard upon your stepdaughter, Mrs. Wickes," Lord Merritt said. "She, too, has suffered."

Slowly and gently, Lord Merritt placed his hand on Rosamunde's shoulder—a small reminder that he was concerned for her well-being, she supposed. As deeply as she hurt inside with concern for her shy stepsister, Rosamunde felt the additional pain of the quandary in which his lordship's presence left her. Was he truly here to comfort her, or merely here to keep an eye on where she went to retrieve that blasted treasure in order to save Mary Ann?

"However shall we save Mary Ann?" Mrs. Wickes demanded. "However shall we convince those horrid men that we have no treasure?"

"How shall we even contact them?" Rosamunde asked.

"I . . . I have a suspicion that they might be found at the Dead Man's Head Inn," Lord Merritt said quietly.

Rosamunde's eyes darkened with confirmed suspicions.

She wanted to hate him completely now, but his treachery hurt too much even to allow that emotion in her heart.

"Then that is where we shall go," she said.

What a wretched smell! Mary Ann thought as she returned to consciousness. Step-papa must be fertilizing the garden once again.

She tried to lift her hand to scratch her nose, but found that her wrists were fastened tightly together. What in heaven's name . . . !

Remembrance dawned upon her with exceeding unpleasantness. Those two horrid men—Raikes and Gidley—even their names were horrid!

Slowly, she opened her eyes and looked about her. Why the wretches had brought her to a filthy barn! They had left her tied up with scratchy, uncomfortable ropes in dirty, smelly hay, with a ragged handkerchief that had come from who knows where tied firmly about her mouth.

Well, she was still alive. Nothing hurt, so she must be well and whole.

She hoped the authorities would catch those awful men—and punish them severely for this. Why, hanging was too good for those two! She wondered if she might be able to convince the authorities to revive drawing and quartering—or at least thumbscrews.

"If ye scream, we'll kill ye outright," Raikes warned her.

Despite her fears, Mary Ann glared at his wrinkled, weather-beaten face.

"We really don't want to kill ye, ye understand," Raikes explained. "Ye'll be worth nothing to us dead, and 'twill be a damned nuisance trying to capture and use that little wildcat Rosamunde for a hostage."

" 'Twould serve you right," Mary Ann tried to tell them, but the coarse white cotton handkerchief muffled most of her words.

"What did ye say?" Raikes asked.

Mary Ann tried to repeat her words.

Gidley moved closer to her. Mary Ann thought she should faint again, but the huge man stopped and merely gestured toward the handkerchief.

"Aye, I suppose ye're right again, Gidley," Raikes acknowledged reluctantly. "If she decided to tell us where the treasure is, how could we understand her with that in her mouth?"

"Ye'll not scream," he ordered Mary Ann. He gave her a warning glare.

Mary Ann shook her head.

Raikes unfastened the rough knot. The cloth dropped into the straw. Mary Ann gasped for a much-needed breath.

"Well, sink me!" Raikes declared. "She didn't scream. Fancy that, a woman who actually keeps her word."

"That is because *I* am a *lady*," Mary Ann informed the filthy little man with a haughtiness which she barely felt.

"Well, little lady," Raikes replied, "will ye be telling us the location o' yer Uncle Peg's treasure so we can send ye home?"

"I have no knowledge of his treasure. *I* was not my uncle's confidante," she answered.

She was trying desperately to maintain her haughty demeanor, yet feared she felt it slipping rapidly away. Oh, no! She must not collapse into hysterics *now*, she decided, and firmly strengthened her waning resolve.

Raikes looked up to Gidley. He stabbed a stubby finger in Mary Ann's direction. "Ye know, for the first time, *this one* I actually believe."

"Anyway, what right have you to the treasure?" Mary Ann demanded.

"Because 'tis truly mine," Raikes said.

"As I recall, the treasure was originally the *Penderricks'*," she reminded them sharply. Merciful heavens! Where had such bravado come from? she wondered.

"Ah," Raikes sighed, settling himself upon a bale of hay in the small barn. "Ye've only heard Peg's version o' the tale. But I'll tell ye what really happened, lass."

Mary Ann had always tried to plead other things to do when Uncle Peg began telling his pirate tales. There was little chance of avoiding one now.

"Ye see, I was the one who found the Penderrick fortune when we boarded the *Dauntless*. That lily-livered little cabin boy, Dudley, he weren't even there, but hid in the bilge during the entire battle."

"He told us he hid under his bunk," Mary Ann corrected.

"Just like Peg to change things about to make himself look better," Raikes grumbled. "At any rate, after *I*'d found the treasure chest for the captain, the thieving scoundrel knocked me over the head, left me for dead, and stole me booty from me. He took Dudley along to do his dirty work when he hid the fortune. 'Twas then and there I vowed revenge."

Well, his revenge was complete as far as she was concerned, Mary Ann decided. They certainly could not have taken her to a more dismal, dirty place!

She shifted about to try to make herself more comfortable in the smelly straw. She could see she was in a small barn, but where? She raised her bound hands to try to rub her itching nose.

"For years I've sailed the Seven Seas, believing all me shipmates dead and the Penderrick fortune at the bottom o' Mounts Bay," Raikes continued. "But not long ago, I learned that the cabin boy o' the *Halverton* had survived that shipwreck. But he'd changed his name—no wonder I hadn't found him before. Now, after all these years, I'll not be cheated out o' me treasure at the eleventh hour."

Mary Ann started at the knock upon the door. Who in the world knocks upon a barn door? she wondered. Who would even come calling at such a late hour?

Raikes cautiously made his way to the door.

"Who be there?" he asked.

"A messenger . . . a bearer of treasure," came the muffled reply through the door.

Mary Ann stifled a gasp. She knew that voice! Oh, what

in heaven's name was *he* doing here? He had no talent for this sort of conflict. He'd only get himself killed, she feared. Yet he said he bore treasure. How could Mr. Shelby have found it? And so quickly?

Cautiously, Raikes opened the door to the dark night outside.

A heavy shovel swung through the doorway, striking Raikes in the face and knocking him unconscious immediately. He fell in a crumpled heap at Mr. Shelby's feet.

Mary Ann screamed as Mr. Shelby leaped over the inert body, swinging the shovel at the enormous Gidley.

Gidley wrenched the shovel from Mr. Shelby's grasp. Seizing both ends of the handle, he snapped the long shaft of wood in half as easily as one might break a twig.

Although he barely came to Gidley's chest, Mr. Shelby, undaunted by size, ducked his head and dove for the giant's middle. He pummeled the man's stomach vigorously with his fists.

Gidley grunted, but remained unaffected. He swung one enormous arm, batting the vicar to the floor as if he were no more significant than a bothersome gnat.

Slowly, Mr. Shelby rose, staggered just a bit, then resumed his attack on Gidley's middle.

Gidley knocked him to the floor again.

"Oh, Mr. Shelby, do stop!" Mary Ann cried. "I fear you are just making him angry."

Wiping a small trickle of blood from the corner of his lip, Mr. Shelby rose again and plunged into the fray, only to be knocked down once again.

He swallowed hard and shook his head, taking a bit longer to rise this time.

"Oh, Mr. Shelby, do stay down!" Mary Ann cried.

But Mr. Shelby was a man obsessed. Once again, he dove for the giant Gidley's midsection.

Gidley's face darkened with anger. While the plump little vicar was wearing himself out in the attack, clearly, Gidley was merely growing weary of this game. With one enormous hand, he seized Mr. Shelby by the cravat and lifted him bodily from the floor.

The vicar's feet dangled beneath him, his face was at last at eye level with his adversary. Gidley glared with hatred at Mr. Shelby while slowly, very slowly, he balled his hand into a ham-sized fist, and drew his arm back to deal Mr. Shelby a finishing blow.

Mary Ann wanted to scream, but could only watch in horror. Gidley knew he had the little man in his power, and he was merely toying with him before landing the strike which would undoubtedly return poor Mr. Shelby to his Maker.

Suddenly Mr. Shelby shot his fist upward, catching Gidley beneath the chin. The man's eyes rolled back in his head, and he collapsed to the ground.

Quite startled, Mr. Shelby stared for some time at his accomplishment. However had he managed to do that? Still and all, he *had* done it. No sense in waiting about until the man came 'round to ask him.

He picked himself up, dusted off his shiny black broadcloth breeches, then wiped his hands together, as if effacing all contact he had ever made with the distasteful pair.

"Oh, Mr. Shelby!" Mary Ann stared up at him in wonder and admiration as Mr. Shelby untied her hands. "Josiah! However did you manage to do that?"

Mr. Shelby glared with disdain upon his fallen adversary. "Quite plainly, the fellow cannot take a facer."

"How brave you are! How strong!" she declared, swooning quite deliberately against his chest. "You saved my life!"

"Why, of course I did. I had to. I . . . I love you, Mary Ann."

"Me?" was all she could manage to say in a high-pitched, squeaky little voice. "Not Rosamunde?"

"Certainly not. Why else do you think I have continued

calling at Eglantine Cottage?" he asked. "You could not seriously believe I came just to eat those wretched little sandwiches your mother makes."

Mary Ann pouted. "*I* made them," she corrected him.

Mr. Shelby turned quite red.

Never would she want to offend him! Quickly, she asked, "However did you find me?"

"Pirates may travel the seas with nary a trail. But upon land," Mr. Shelby said with a disdainful sniff, "those two were more easily tracked than a herd of elephants stampeding down Pall Mall."

"But the treasure! Did they find it? You said you were the bearer—"

"Of treasure? Indeed." Mr. Shelby opened his jacket to reveal his copy of the Bible.

"Oh." Mary Ann was barely able to conceal her disappointment.

"Treasure means different things to different men," he explained.

Ashamed of her initial reaction, Mary Ann smiled at him sheepishly.

"Come, Mary Ann." He bent down and scooped her up in his arms. "I cannot discern when they will regain consciousness, but I, for one, do not want to be here when they do."

He carried her across Raikes' inert body and out the door. "You see," he said. "I did not lie. I am, indeed, bearing what is also treasure to me."

Mary Ann was utterly delighted to hear he considered her thus, for she had always thought that of him.

Once outside, he gently placed her upon the ground but did not release her from his embrace. Instead, he pulled her more closely to him.

Although she had always liked his personality, Mary Ann had heretofore not considered Mr. Shelby to be what one might term vigorous, nor robust, nor even particularly athletic. Yet as he grasped her to him, she felt his unexpected firmness and strength.

He placed a fervent kiss upon her soft, pink lips.

"Why, Josiah," Mary Ann said breathlessly after he released her. "I . . . I had no idea you had such . . . such physical prowess!"

═THIRTEEN═

"What do you mean, 'we'?" Lord Merritt asked Rosamunde.

His icy blue eyes frowned down upon her, causing a flutter deep inside. Oh, she did *not* want to feel that sensation—not about Lord Merritt, not now!

Rosamunde thought that, someday, she might be able to forgive Lord Merritt his abuse of her uncle's friendship—after all, Uncle Peg was dead now, and beyond his lordship's reach. She might let pass his lordship's attempt to draw Sir Polly into his despicable plot—after all, he *was* just a bird. Rosamunde would even forget his lordship's callous abuse of the tender feelings toward him which had grown within her—eventually. But the man had endangered helpless, innocent, and ignorant Mary Ann—and that was the outside of enough!

From the turmoil of emotions which he caused to broil within her, Rosamunde summoned the strength to stare at him defiantly.

"I mean precisely what I said, Lord Merritt. If you are going to the Dead Man's Head Inn to meet Raikes and Gidley, then I am going with you."

"*Roger* will come with me," Lord Merritt said. "You will stay here, where I know you are safe."

"How can you be so certain that I shall be safe here?" she demanded.

"Oh, she's quite correct there, Merritt," Roger interjected.

Rosamunde looked at Mr. Whitlaw with dismay. She was, as yet, uncertain of the man's part in this imbroglio. What knowledge had he of Lord Merritt's plan that he should be convinced of where their safety or peril lay?

Still and all, the man's face had a decidedly pale cast. Perhaps he, too, was his lordship's innocent dupe.

"Suppose Raikes and Gidley decide to come here in search of the treasure?" Roger offered. His brown eyes grew very wide. "I should stay here to protect Mr. and Mrs. Wickes."

Lord Merritt tightened his lips, as if contemplating his alternatives.

"I really should, Merritt," Roger insisted.

His lordship threw up his hands in resignation. "Do as you see fit, Roger. I shall be at the Dead Man's Head Inn."

Lord Merritt turned toward the door. Rosamunde followed him.

He stopped and glared at her. "You are serious," he said. "You truly intend to accompany me."

"You said we may do as we see fit," she answered. "I am coming with you."

Lord Merritt passed his hand across his squared chin. Then, without another word, he continued toward the door. Rosamunde followed close behind.

Suddenly Sir Polly lifted from his perch and swooped through the sitting room to land on Rosamunde's shoulder.

"Shoo!" she cried. "I cannot take you!"

"Hoist anchor, ye lily-livered swab!" Sir Polly would not be moved.

" 'Tis too dangerous," she protested, shaking her shoulder to try to unseat him.

"Belay that bilge, ye black-hearted trollop!" Sir Polly flapped his wings and held on all the more tightly.

Rosamunde stopped her efforts to rid herself of her unwanted companion. "Sir Polly, it appears you leave me no alternative," she reluctantly acknowledged.

Lord Merritt took a step backward and bowed with

exaggerated graciousness as he allowed Rosamunde to precede him out the cottage door. He came up close behind her and whispered, "Now you, too, know what it is like to be saddled with an unwanted companion."

His breath upon the back of her neck caused little shivers to run up her spine—and not, she knew full well, from the tension of the situation, but rather from the nearness of the man himself.

Fighting down her feelings, she turned to him. The most self-satisfied smirk—indeed, it was a smirk, she decided—spread across Lord Merritt's face.

Not so long ago, she had been glad to see his rare smile. Why, then, did it bother her so now? And why had a man as obviously obstinate as his lordship accepted her presence so readily? Did he intend to keep her under his surveillance in case she went to retrieve the nonexistent treasure in order to ransom Mary Ann? Could he know that she herself was intent upon seeing that he did not harm Mary Ann when no treasure was forthcoming?

Attempting to ignore Lord Merritt's remark, Rosamunde advised Sir Polly, "If you intend to stay with me, you had best be quiet."

Lord Merritt tucked his finger beneath her chin and lifted her face to his. His icy blue eyes gleamed. "You, too," he warned.

By the time Rosamunde recovered her wits, Lord Merritt had already swung into his horse's saddle. Looking down upon her from his great height, he said, "If you intend to come with me, you had best mount up."

"We have no horse," she said. Surely the man knew that much about her family's impoverished condition.

He reached down, offering her his hand.

"Oh, dear," Rosamunde muttered to herself. "How to accomplish this?"

Even though she stood upon the mounting block, she needed to raise her skirt so that she could put her foot in the stirrup which he had left empty for her. She reached up to grasp his hand. Blast the man! He was still grinning at her. As much as she tried, she could not fight down the color which rose to her face when she realized that he had a clearly unobstructed view of her ankle, her calf—who knew what else?

'Ah, well. I do it to save Mary Ann,' she reasoned, rather proud of her own nobility of spirit in this trying circumstance.

With very little effort, his lordship swung her up to sit pillion behind him. Sir Polly squawked and flapped his protest, yet never lost his perch. Quickly, Rosamunde smoothed down her rumpled skirts.

"Put your arms about my waist," he told her.

She hesitated. How pleasant the sensation would have been to her not so long ago. Now? Why, she had no intention of coming into such intimate contact with his perfidious lordship now!

When she hesitated, Lord Merritt said, "I would not want you to fall."

Still, she did not comply. "Why not?" she asked sarcastically. "Then you should be rid of me."

Very softly, his lordship replied, "I never said I wanted to be rid of you."

She was about to protest that, indeed, his lordship had made it quite clear that he did not want her, when she suddenly realized that he was correct. All he had said was that he did not want her to accompany him now.

She allowed herself to wrap her arms about his waist. Not very tightly, of course, just enough to insure her own safety riding with this peculiar man.

Peculiar, perhaps . . . but warm, she added to her assessment of him as they rode along. Strong and hard—his muscles tense as he guided the galloping horse toward their destination. Yet somehow soft, as well. Not the pudgy softness of fellows who sat, night and day, eating and drinking over their card games, but a thin veneer of relaxed muscle which overlay the firmness beneath, making her want to hold him all the more closely to her.

'Oh, have mercy!' she released a silent wail. 'I'm supposed to hate this man!'

Rosamunde reluctantly released him as he reined his horse to a halt in front of the Dead Man's Head Inn.

"M'lord, what an honor you do us!" the innkeeper exclaimed as they entered. Bowing obsequiously, he showed them to a table by the door. "Please forgive our lack of private accommodations for yourself and the lady."

The inn was dark, illuminated by only a few tallow candles. Rosamunde blinked away the tears that the smoke from the badly drawing fire brought to her eyes.

Lord Merritt indicated that Rosamunde should sit upon the rough-hewn bench. Then he took the seat across from her.

"How may I serve your lordship? A pint of our finest ale? A meat pasty for yourself and the lady?" He leaned closer to Lord Merritt and his voice dropped in volume. "I've some very fine French brandy just recently arrived . . ."

Lord Merritt waved away all his suggestions. "I was told that a Mr. Raikes and his business associate, Mr. Gidley, are staying here."

"You've been misinformed, m'lord," the innkeeper said, drawing himself erect and glancing about nervously. "I know naught of such men. Now, what about a nice—"

"One is an elderly, wizened fellow," his lordship explained as he withdrew a shilling from his waistcoat pocket and placed it before him on the table. With studied nonchalance, he toyed with the shiny disk. "The other, a silent giant of a man." Slowly, he pushed the coin toward the innkeeper.

"Well, m'lord," the innkeeper said, reaching out hesitantly, " 'tis hard to keep account of all the comings and goings of the patrons of this inn. If I had a moment to think . . ."

"Certainly." Lord Merritt withdrew another shilling and

pushed it toward the innkeeper, who snatched both up immediately.

"Indeed, two such fellows were here," the innkeeper said as the sound of the two clinking coins falling into his pocket jogged his flagging memory. "Now, as to their where-abouts . . ."

Lord Merritt offered a final coin.

"I truly do not know. They left late this afternoon. As a matter of fact, they left through the kitchen door, as they appeared to be wanting to avoid that gentleman over there." The innkeeper nodded toward the darkest corner of the taproom.

Rosamunde had not noticed the man before. It was the unidentified man who had come to the house after Uncle Peg's funeral. She suppressed a small gasp of surprise.

Quite casually, Lord Merritt turned around in his chair. He exhibited no such surprise.

The man knew that he had been seen. Slowly, he rose and moved toward the doorway. As he passed them, he nodded politely to Rosamunde.

"Good evening, Miss Wickes."

He nodded to his lordship as well.

Not so unusual, she decided, until the man said, "Good evening, Lord Merritt."

Who was this man? She still did not know his name. What was he doing here? If Raikes and Gidley were seeking to avoid him, she puzzled, how could he be a pirate in league with them? He obviously knew Lord Merritt and was not avoiding *him*. Could he be working for his lordship? If he was in Lord Merritt's employ and Raikes and Gidley wanted to avoid him, then how could his lordship still be in league with Raikes and Gidley?

Rosamunde shook the swirling questions from her head. She was too concerned right now with saving Mary Ann. She did not need this additional worry. Blast Lord Merritt for confusing her so!

The door closed behind the rotund man.

Rosamunde leaned forward over the table. "You know that man," she accused. "Who is he?"

He brought his face much closer to her as well. In the darkness of the room, his pale blue eyes seemed to shine with an inner light.

"I presumed him to be an associate of Raikes and Gidley," Lord Merritt replied slowly, almost, Rosamunde thought, evasively.

Suddenly, Lord Merritt rose. "We must leave here. Now." Grasping her hand, he pulled Rosamunde to her feet and fairly dragged her to the tap where the innkeeper stood.

"Would you be so kind as to show us the door by which Mr. Raikes and Mr. Gidley departed?" his lordship requested.

The innkeeper nodded toward the rugged door behind him.

"Why are we going this way?" Rosamunde asked as Lord Merritt pulled her along through the murky kitchen. "Do you think they left some indication of where they went?"

Lord Merritt shook his head. "We could never be that lucky. But I have a strange feeling that Raikes and Gidley are not the only two people that man is watching."

Just past the dilapidated barn behind the shabby little inn, they encountered a small black carriage.

"That's it!" Rosamunde cried. Drawing up sharply, she squeezed Lord Merritt's hand in excitement. "That's the carriage they used when they kidnapped Mary Ann."

"Are you quite certain?" Lord Merritt asked, frowning. "After all, one dark carriage looks pretty much like another."

"Oh, I would not forget this one," she assured him.

"That is good."

"That is horrible!" Rosamunde contradicted him. "Have you any idea the nightmares I shall have recalling those two beastly men chasing me in this horrid carriage?"

"If the carriage is still here," Lord Merritt explained, "then Raikes and Gidley are still in the area, too."

"They could have left by foot or astride," Rosamunde offered, fearful that they truly had gone, taking Mary Ann with them.

Lord Merritt shook his head. "They need the coach to travel with Mary Ann. She would attract too much notice otherwise."

The renewed hope Lord Merritt gave her for Mary Ann's eventual recovery eased some of the tension from her shoulders. She sighed with relief and unwittingly relaxed against his strong shoulder.

Rosamunde released a small chuckle. "Mary Ann could not attract attention if she were painted bright blue."

Lord Merritt stared at her. One corner of his fine lips twitched as it curved upward. In spite of her concern, Rosamunde found herself smiling back at him.

At the same time, they both realized their intimate contact and the fact that he still held her hand.

Quickly, she backed away from him, her fingers slipping slowly from his. Lord Merritt's strong fingers clung to hers a moment before he reluctantly released her from his grasp. He moved his empty hand back and forth beside him several times, almost as if to take her hand again. Then, instead, he reached up and stroked his chin.

Rosamunde fondly noted the familiar gesture. Then she shook her head sharply, as if that would also shake the grin from her lips and her warm—and at this point unwished for—thoughts of Lord Merritt from her mind. She did not want to allow herself to think of anything about that untrustworthy gentleman with any emotion even remotely resembling affection.

Lord Merritt was closing the barn door. He turned back to her, shaking his head. "She's not in there." Then he asked, more of himself than of Rosamunde, "but where have they taken her?"

How Rosamunde wished she knew!

"Come." Lord Merritt reached out to grab her hand once

again, obviously thought better of it, and merely repeated, "Come with me."

"Where?"

"The tin mines."

"Are you mad?" she demanded. "Uncle Peg warned us to stay away from the mines."

"Indeed," Lord Merritt replied, his silvery-blue eyes alight. " 'Tis a good place to hide."

Lord Merritt *had* to go to Penderrick Keep. He could not tackle the mine, or Raikes and Gidley, with no weapons and no light. Lord Merritt could only hope that Fickle would be as resourceful in digging up lanterns and perhaps a pistol or fowling piece as he had been in turning up all his relatives.

Yet his lordship approached the place reluctantly. He did not want Rosamunde to see the once-lovely estate now in ruins. How he wished she had stayed behind, safe at Eglantine Cottage!

His lordship gave a rueful chuckle under his breath. He had little choice in the matter. Rosamunde was determined to accompany him, no matter where he went. He hoped—indeed, it was very important to him—that she would understand that, usually, he *never* allowed his places of residence to look so unkempt.

Yet, as they approached Penderrick Keep, the candlelight streaming through the windows across the neatly clipped expanse of lawn was bright and inviting. Even in the dark, Lord Merritt noticed the gravel drive had been smoothed.

As he reined his horse to a halt before the entrance, a dark-haired young man appeared from the shadows to take his horse by the bridle.

"Who are you?" his lordship demanded, refusing to relinquish the reins.

"I'm the groom, m'lord," he prompted Lord Merritt's memory. "Fickle's cousin."

"Oh, indeed."

Rosamunde leaned closer against him. He could feel her warm breath on the back of his neck.

"Don't you even know your own people, my lord?" she asked.

She must think him the veriest fool! Lord Merritt thought with consternation. Then he heard her soft laugh. This time, he did not even bother to try to suppress the grin which rose to his lips.

The groom held his horse's head while he dismounted, then assisted Rosamunde down.

Lord Merritt had the distinct feeling that he should not leave his expensive steed in the care of this strange man. After all, hadn't his mother been accused of consorting with . . . ?

With slight alarm, he observed that Raikes', Gidley's, and Childers' furtive skulkings had certainly shaken his own usually unruffled demeanor.

'You're going mad, Merritt,' he told himself. 'You're becoming as peculiar as Fickle and Peg and everyone else around here!'

Fickle threw open the door to greet him. With a lingering hesitancy, Lord Merritt escorted Rosamunde into the hall.

The myriad candles in several recently reappeared candelabra shone in the highly polished wood of the paneled walls and parquetry floor. His lordship had absolutely no idea where the rest of the furnishings came from—and he was not about to ask. The only trouble with the entire picture was the flock of children that ranged up and down the hall, rolling hoops, pulling carts, dragging dolls.

"Terrence!" Lord Merritt exclaimed upon spotting the one and only short person whom he could identify. "Where did all these toys come from?"

"Oh, m'lord, this isn't all of them!" the boy exclaimed. "There's ever so many more up in the nursery."

"Do you not think that is where they should remain?"

"But, m'lord, you only said to keep my ball out of Penderrick Keep," Terrence protested. He swung his arm out to indicate the hall, almost striking his lordship in the stomach. "See, m'lord. There's not a ball in here!"

Lord Merritt was just about to scold his miniature nemesis when he heard Rosamunde laugh.

He turned to her. He watched the pale skin of her cheeks turn rosy pink with laughter. Her large gray-blue eyes crinkled softly at the corners. There was a small crease near the tip of her nose he had never noticed before. But then, he had never seen her laughing this heartily before.

The poor condition of the house did not seem to bother her. Nor did the scattered toys and boisterous children. Why, the lady almost appeared to be enjoying them. And, if the truth be owned, Lord Merritt found, much to his surprise, that he rather enjoyed it, too.

"You are indeed a man of your word, Terrence," Lord Merritt pronounced with a smile. "In the future, do try to keep wheeled conveyances out of the hall as well."

The children seized their toys and scattered.

"Oh, Lord Merritt," Rosamunde now managed to gasp between subsiding giggles. "If only . . . if only you could have seen the look on your face . . . !" Quite out of breath, she began to sit on the long, ruggedly made bench.

"Don't sit there!" his lordship cried, making a lunge for her. Seizing her up in his arms, he stopped her from sitting on the wobbly bench that had been Roger's undoing.

Her soft breasts crushed against his chest. She made no attempt to push away from him, but instead held the sleeves of his jacket tightly. Her eyes, which only moments ago had been drawn up in laughter, were now wide with surprise. Not only surprise, his lordship noted as he continued to stand there holding her close to him. There was—dare he believe it?—a look of anticipation on her face. He wondered if his own anticipation was as evident. And he wondered if Rosamunde was anticipating the same thing that was on his mind.

"We found plenty of lanterns in the cellar, m'lord,"

Fickle declared. He and one of his cousins, each bearing lanterns, stomped noisily into the hall. "Oh, don't let *me* interrupt anything, m'lord!"

Quickly, Lord Merritt released Rosamunde and stepped back several paces. "I was merely trying to prevent Miss Wickes from taking a spill if she sat upon that bench," he said gruffly.

"Oh, 'tis nothing amiss with this bench, m'lord." Fickle settled himself with ease upon the quite steady bench.

There most certainly had been earlier, his lordship protested silently. Blast! If Rosamunde should think he had feigned damage to the bench just to hold her in his arms . . .

Lord Merritt cleared his throat. "I . . . I assume your brother-in-law completed his repairs."

"Well, of course, m'lord!" Fickle declared. "We wouldn't want our visitors doing themselves a damage, would we?"

"Of course not." Quickly, Lord Merritt took one of the rusted lanterns and examined it with what he knew—but hoped no one else noticed—was overly solicitous scrutiny.

"Are you certain you don't want us to come with you, m'lord?" Fickle asked eagerly.

"Thank you, but no. Our best tactic is to take them by surprise. I shall manage that alone."

"You don't appear to be alone, m'lord," Fickle said to his lordship, all the while grinning at Rosamunde.

"As I propose to rescue her stepsister, the lady is most essential to my plan," Lord Merritt explained. Oh, why the deuce should he feel the need to explain anything to his butler, for heaven's sake?

"Oh, I'm sure she is," Fickle responded.

Turning his attention to the lanterns, his lordship asked sharply, "Fickle, are these in working order?"

"Oh, yes, m'lord. However, the only thing I could find here by way of weapons was this." From behind his back

Fickle withdrew a small, ancient rapier and brandished it about.

"Where on earth . . . ?"

"I found it in one of the empty bedchambers, m'lord," Fickle answered, fencing awkwardly about the hall. "I was polishing it to hang over the mantel in the drawing room until more suitable ornamentation could be found. 'Twas intended as a surprise, m'lord."

"Very kind of you, Fickle," his lordship acknowledged. He held out his hand. Reluctantly, Fickle relinquished his weapon.

Lord Merritt flexed the steel, then assumed an easy, ready stance.

"Oh, Lord Merritt," Rosamunde said in a low voice. "You do not actually intend to use that, do you?"

"I sincerely hope I do not need to."

=FOURTEEN=

Rosamunde and Lord Merritt peered cautiously into the dark hole. The other mine openings they had found were all caved in, their enginehouses in ruins. But, although the tall brick tower of this mine's enginehouse had crumbled and its timber engine beam was rapidly rotting away in the damp sea air, this portal was still open, and wide enough for a man to enter easily. Equally important, it had a ladder.

However, the lantern light only illuminated the rickety wooden ladder a short way as it disappeared down into the darkness of the shaft.

Rosamunde strained to listen, turning her left ear. "There is nothing down there."

"Are you so certain?" Lord Merritt asked, his eyebrow raised inquisitively. Rosamunde might also have said suspiciously. "Suppose they left Mary Ann down there alone . . . injured?"

Now it was Rosamunde's turn to study Lord Merritt suspiciously.

"Then you must go down," she told him.

"I?"

"I surely cannot retrieve her myself."

"I do not think there is room for me."

"But I have Sir Polly." She nodded to the bird who still clung stubbornly to her shoulder.

Did Lord Merritt suspect she was trying to leave him down the hole so that she could retrieve the treasure and ransom Mary Ann? Rosamunde wondered. Was that why he wanted her to go? Or was he trying to leave her there, a hostage as well?

Rosamunde and Lord Merritt stood, alternately peering into the hole and assessing each other.

"Oh, this will never do! We are wasting precious time." Rosamunde's patience had exceeded its limits. "I shall go, but you must come with me."

"*With* you?" he repeated.

"We shall descend together."

Once again, he peered down the dark hole. "Do you think that ladder will hold us?"

"If Gidley went down, it will certainly hold the two of us."

Lord Merritt grinned at her as he stepped aside and bowed. "You first, Miss Wickes."

"Oh, no, my lord," she demurred with an equally polite curtsey. All the while she continued to watch him suspiciously. "After you."

"I would but for the fact that, should I look upward in the descent—and being merely human," he added with a wicked rise of his eyebrow, "and subject to base, physical temptations, I do not think I could resist—I believe I should encounter a breathtaking view."

Rosamunde lowered her lantern so that Lord Merritt could not see her blush.

She was also exceedingly glad that he could not see her on the way down. Her face, indeed her entire body, was warm. Did Lord Merritt think that, unlike his lordship, *she* was incapable of succumbing to base, physical temptations?

Of course, she could not help but notice how the buff-colored inexpressibles fit so nicely to the back of his muscular thigh, and molded up the curve of his hip, and smoothed snugly over his firm . . . oh, merciful heavens!

Rosamunde reached the bottom and moved quickly back for Lord Merritt to dismount from the ladder.

Rosamunde and Lord Merritt held their lanterns high in order to examine their surroundings. Large baulks of rotting timber shored up the walls of the shaft. One had fallen to the floor of the mine shaft. A disused and rusting balance bob, detached from the main pump rod it once counterbalanced, faded into the darkness.

Suddenly, Sir Polly left Rosamunde's shoulder for a perch upon a fallen timber.

"Well, thank you, at last," Rosamunde remarked to her feathered companion. She rubbed her aching shoulder. "You're deucedly heavy after a while, you know."

"Avast! I thought ye'd never go down that bloody ladder!" Raikes' voice cried down to them. "Now bring us up the treasure."

"There is no treasure down here," Lord Merritt answered.

"Why should we be believing yer lordship?"

Why should they not? Rosamunde wondered. Why had his lordship so readily volunteered the information if they were *not* working together?

"Where is Mary Ann?" Rosamunde called up to them.

There was no answer.

"Where is my sister?" she demanded.

"We . . . we need the treasure first," Raikes replied.

"I'll not hand it over until I know Mary Ann is safe." Merciful heavens! What was she saying? There was no treasure, yet here she was, striking bargains with ruthless pirates.

"She be safe, o' that ye can be sure."

"Am I to take *your* word for it?" she asked scornfully.

She heard some furtive whispering from above, but could not discern what was being said.

Suddenly the ladder shuddered and loosened from its shorings in the mine wall. It began to rise.

Rosamunde screamed. Lord Merritt lunged for the rapidly ascending ladder. He managed to grasp the last rung, but one wrench from the powerful Gidley pulled it abruptly from his lordship's strong grip.

Raikes held his lantern over the side. In the dancing light

and shadows of the flame, his wizened face appeared to be that of a veritable demon. And what on earth had happened to his nose? It looked slightly bent and decidedly purple.

"I'll give ye one last chance to disclose the location o' the treasure."

"Not until I have Mary Ann!" Rosamunde cried defiantly.

"Drop the ladder, Raikes," Lord Merritt commanded.

"I can't do that, m'lord," he answered. "I'll just be leaving ye both here 'til ye can tell me where the treasure be." With that, Raikes disappeared.

As they made their way through the darkness, Raikes said to his silent companion, "We had to be leaving them there. We can't tell them we don't know where Mary Ann is any more than they do. After all, what kind o' pirates lose their captive to the *vicar*?"

Gidley nodded in grim agreement.

"Well, you've got me in the suds now!" Rosamunde complained. Sighing, she settled herself beside Sir Polly at one end of the fallen timber.

"I've got *you*?" Lord Merritt repeated incredulously. Heedless of the dirt and damp, he sat beside Rosamunde on the beam.

" 'Twas *you* who sent me down here," she snapped.

"As I recall, you wanted *me* to go."

"Because *you* told me Mary Ann might be down here."

"It was your idea that we both go," Lord Merritt reminded her testily. "If I had been above, I could have stopped them . . ."

"Or left me down here alone while you three made off . . ."

"How *dare* you think I'm working with those despicable—"

" 'Twas *your* idea to come to the tin mines in the first place. Uncle Peg warned you away from them."

"I thought this was where he might have hidden the treasure."

"I'm sick of your search for that blasted treasure!" she shouted. She sprang to her feet and stood over Lord Merritt, glaring down at him. "I want to know where my sister is!"

Lord Merritt slowly rose from the fallen timber. He stood so close that their bodies almost touched. "I don't know where she is. How can you think I might know where she is and not tell you?"

Rosamunde lowered her gaze. "I don't. Not any more," she murmured. "Else why would they leave you here, too?"

She waited for a reply, yet Lord Merritt said nothing. Well, this was as close as she could manage to an apology after the extremely suspicious manner in which his lordship had conducted himself. If the man was waiting for more abject penitence, he could just stand there—but must he stand so disturbingly close?

"At any rate," his lordship said, startling her as he broke the silence which enveloped them. He slowly moved to the side, breaking the invisible contact between them. "I do not think they have Mary Ann any longer."

She eyed him with renewed suspicion. "If you are not in their confidence, how can you know they do not have her?"

"If they still had Mary Ann, they would not need to hold us for the information."

Rosamunde was still skeptical. "You only say that to make me feel better."

"I would not say that just to make you feel better."

"Oh, thank you so much," she shot back sarcastically.

"I did not mean . . ." He placed his hand upon her shoulder.

"I know you did not," she said softly.

It was rather comforting to realize that Lord Merritt was not working with the pirates. But, my gracious! How his nearness still had the power to unsettle her.

Slowly, she moved away. "I do see your reasoning, my lord. I only hope you are right."

She sat again upon the timber. She tried her best to suppress a sob, but only ended up shuddering.

"It's just, I am so worried about Mary Ann," she explained, shaking her head slowly. "She has always been such a timid little thing. Why, she faints at the very mention of blood. What would she do if she were truly frightened? How will she survive being kidnapped by those two horrid men?"

"I would wager she will not do what you do," Lord Merritt replied.

"What do I do?"

"You get angry and shout at people who are merely trying to help," he told her.

In the flickering lantern light, Rosamunde could see the teasing grin which played across his lips and the merriment which danced in his eyes.

"And just what are you doing to help?" she challenged him.

"Well, I shall simply have to climb out of here."

"My lord, Raikes and Gidley took the ladder," she reminded him. "Unless you carry another ladder secreted about your person?"

Recalling those blasted skintight inexpressibles, she highly doubted that he did. Oh, how could she have phrased her supposedly clever little remark in quite such an embarrassing manner!

"I shall not need a ladder."

He handed her the ancient rapier. Stripping off his jacket, he threw it carelessly over the fallen timber.

He began to scratch about the dirt walls of the mine shaft. He dug his well-manicured hands into the dirt side of the shaft and began to pull himself up. He stuck the toe of each once-shining boot into the hole that was left after he removed his hand.

"Oh, do be careful, Lord Merritt," Rosamunde pleaded.

He cursed as the damp soil crumbled away beneath his

fingers and he slipped back to the bottom. Undaunted, he tried again.

Breathless, Rosamunde watched him mount higher and higher along the sheer wall of the mine shaft. About halfway up, he slipped, grabbed frantically into the dirt for purchase, then tumbled into a heap, striking the beam with his arm as he landed.

"Oh, Lord Merritt," Rosamunde cried, rushing to his side. She held his arm, assisting him to rise.

"I'm fine. Truly, I am," he protested, rising and brushing off his dusty seat, taking care to use only his uninjured arm.

"You most certainly are not." Rosamunde pointed to the blood which seeped into the fabric of his shirt sleeve.

" 'Tis a mere scratch—"

"Nonsense," she said to quiet his protest. She pointed upward. "*There* you may be a viscount, but *here*, you are my patient. Now sit." She indicated a seat on the fallen beam.

She turned her back to him, lifted the skirt of her gown and began to tear a long narrow strip from the hem of her petticoat.

She knelt at his feet and placed his arm, injured side up, upon his leg. Carefully lifting the torn edges, she ripped his shirt sleeve up to the elbow.

His blood matted the short strands of sandy-colored hair which curled lightly across his forearm. Gingerly, she dabbed at the wound with an edge of clean fabric. She released a small sigh of relief. Already the blood had stopped flowing and was beginning to clot.

Slowly and carefully, she wrapped the strip of bandage about his forearm.

She looked up into his eyes. He was looking down upon her in the strangest manner. Indeed, there was a softness about his lordship's eyes that belied the gravity of their situation. Merciful heavens! Was his lordship suffering some sort of shock which would make him want to stay here?

Suddenly his lordship broke their gaze. Slapping his undamaged hand at his side, he again approached the wall.

"Surely, you cannot mean to . . ."

"Oh, yes. I must," he answered her protest.

He dug his fingers in, more slowly this time. Rosamunde winced in sympathy for the pain he must be enduring.

Once again, he fell to the floor of the mine, bringing a heavy shower of dirt and rocks down upon them both. Even before his lordship could touch the wall again, more dirt cascaded down upon them.

"I dare not try again," he said breathlessly. He sat dejectedly upon the beam. "One more attempt will undoubtedly collapse the shaft, suffocating us."

"If we do not climb out, we shall starve to death down here," Rosamunde said as she sat beside him. Her voice sounded strangely flat, as if she had already accepted their fate.

"Deucedly limited choices, wouldn't you say?"

Rosamunde nodded.

"We shall wait," Lord Merritt suggested. "Perhaps when we do not return, your family will recall Peg's warnings about the mines."

"I highly doubt it," Rosamunde said with a sigh of resignation. "They never paid attention to anything else he said."

They stared silently into the waning light of the lantern.

At length, Rosamunde said, "I have heard people say that in some mines there are poison gases which can kill a person without their even being aware."

"You truly have a delightful talent for light conversation, Miss Wickes," his lordship said with a chuckle.

She cast him a worried look.

He placed his arm about her shoulder to comfort her. "Of course there are no poison gases here. If there were, Sir Polly would be dead by now."

"Sir Polly!" Rosamunde cried. She sprang to her feet and

rushed to the parrot's side. "We shall have him fly out and alert the family."

Lord Merritt shook his head in dismay. "You have been reading far too many romance novels. That sort of thing never *really* happens."

"You've no imagination, my lord," Rosamunde scolded.

"But, is it not usually a dog which . . . ?"

"Oh, pooh. Sir Polly can do anything a mere canine can do," Rosamunde asserted. Her spirits somewhat revived, she turned confidently to Sir Polly. "Good Sir Polly, fly off now. Shoo! Shoo!" She waved her arms before him.

"All hands confined to quarters," Sir Polly replied.

Rosamunde waved her arms more frantically. "Shoo! Shoo!"

Sir Polly remained impassive.

Rosamunde drew a bit closer to the uncooperative parrot and whispered, "Sir Polly, you are making us both look extraordinarily foolish in front of his lordship."

Still, he could not be coerced.

"Sir Polly, knighted for bravery? My great-aunt Sally's drawers!" she grumbled as she returned to her seat on the timber beside Lord Merritt. "What kind of hero are you?"

Her shoulders hunched, her hands clasped in her lap, Rosamunde stared at the floor of the mine shaft. She heaved a heavy sigh and shivered in the murky dampness.

Without saying a word, Lord Merritt placed his jacket about her shoulders. She shivered as her body tried to draw in all the warmth that his body had imparted to the cloth.

Silently, he slid closer to her and placed his arm about her shoulder. She did not protest. He ventured to draw her nearer, just as he had held her on the night Peg had passed away. How unbelievably odd to think that if someone did not find them soon, they would be two of the dearly departed as well. And perhaps no one would ever know what had happened to them.

"Well," Rosamunde said length, "I suppose we shall both die here."

"Oh, no, Miss Wickes—" Lord Merritt began to protest.

"Oh, you mustn't lie to me or cajole me as one might a child," she said in a quiet, dull voice. "I'm old enough to know the truth. And, after all those visits from Mr. Shelby, and all those dreary Thursday afternoons doing good at the Misses Randolph's society, I suppose I'm as ready to meet my Maker as anyone could be."

He really should stop her morbid musings, Lord Merritt decided. Yet how? Indeed, with her small shoulders tucked under his arms and her softly scented hair tickling his cheek, one method of distracting her sprang immediately to his mind. However, in view of the circumstances, he did not think the lady might readily comply. As there was little else to do down here, he merely sat close to her and listened.

"Still and all, I should like to have lived to a ripe old age," she continued. "But most of all, I regret that I never had any grand adventures."

"What, may I ask, do you consider *this*?" he asked incredulously.

"This? This is not an adventure. This is a bloody nuisance," she answered. "I have spent my life in Penzance, and now, when all is said and done, I shall truly be stuck forever in Penzance. In a bloody mine shaft in Penzance, of all places. Oh, blast this mine! Oh, blast Penzance!" She stamped both feet angrily for emphasis.

She sat there silently for a moment as her frustration subsided. From out of the corner of her eye, she glanced over to Lord Merritt. Perhaps she had been rather selfish with all her ranting and raving, she decided. After all, his lordship was in the same fix. She turned to face him.

"You're a person of far more consequence than I, my lord. I'm sure you had plans for more important things than getting trapped in an abandoned mine shaft during a brief trip to Penzance," she said sheepishly.

Lord Merritt studied the tips of his boots for a moment. How could he confide in this sensitive lady the greatest regret in his life thus far? Looking at her innocent gray-blue eyes looking up at him in curious anticipation, how could he not?

"My greatest regret," he began, "is that I was not able to recover the Penderrick fortune—"

"Oh, blast that bloody fortune, too!" she declared, her anger revived. She gave his lordship a shove that nearly sent him flying from his seat. "'Tis what got us here in the first place. I wish I'd never heard of the wretched thing. I wish I'd never had the misfortune to encounter you, either, you callous greedy monster! Haven't you enough wealth? Must you go chasing across England for more, making poor, innocent people like my family and me miserable in the process? How can you be so selfish?"

Her tirade finally finished, Rosamunde crossed her arms over her breast and emphatically turned her back upon his most-avaricious lordship.

Lord Merritt watched her as the glow of the lantern light sent shots of gold through her dark hair. She thought him greedy and selfish. That pained him more than he could have believed possible. And, more than he could have believed, he wanted to correct the completely erroneous impression she had formed of him.

"Miss Wickes," he said softly.

She did not reply.

"Rosamunde," he said as he placed his hand upon her shoulder.

This time she turned about.

"Do you truly think me so terrible?"

She gave her head a sharp nod.

"Is there nothing I can say to change your opinion of me?"

"I cannot see what, my lord."

"Then I must tell you, I do not seek the treasure for myself. I seek it for my mother."

Rosamunde gave a little sniff and turned slightly away from him. "Your mother has been dead many years, my lord. I do not think she will be much availing herself of your generous efforts."

"For my mother's *sake*, then," Lord Merritt corrected. "Had the Penderrick fortunes not been lost, I would not have been born."

"Ah, yet another reason for regret," Rosamunde remarked sarcastically.

"When the dowerless Gwenyth Penderrick wed the wealthy John Edmonds, Lord Merritt, everyone thought it an exceptionally good match. What they could not know— what no one knows to this day—is that she was cruelly beaten and abused. When she failed to appear socially because her bruises so marred her appearance, my father passed it off as delicate health, and everyone believed him. No one but myself and a few discreet servants knew the true cause of her suffering."

The quavering timbre of his lordship's voice caused Rosamunde to forget her imperious posture. She uncrossed her arms and turned to him, intent upon his story.

"Had she a dowry, she might have made a better marriage. Surely she could not have made a worse," he said with a slow, sad shake of his head. " 'Tis foolish, I know, but somehow I think that perhaps if I could restore the Penderrick fortune, I might vindicate my mother's sad life." He looked directly into her eyes. "Do you understand?"

"Yes, I do now," she said softly, returning his steady gaze.

Oh, bother! What a horrendous harridan she must appear, thinking such terrible things about Lord Merritt, when all the time he had a perfectly unselfish reason for his quest.

Filled with remorse, she gently placed her hand atop his. "I am sorry for your mother. I should have known . . ."

"How could you?" he asked, covering her small hand with his own. "No one knows, not even Roger. I have never told anyone—but you."

Rosamunde took a deep breath. "I should have known . . . that I could not feel this way about you . . ."

Although his arm ached, Lord Merritt lifted it and slowly moved his hand until it rested upon her shoulder.

"How could I have been so mistaken?" she asked.

Still gazing intently into her eyes, Lord Merritt slid his hand about her slender neck and entwined his fingers in her thick, dark curls. He drew her closer to him. She offered no resistance as his lips descended on hers.

══FIFTEEN══

"Rosamunde, how I've wanted to hold you," he murmured. "To touch you. To kiss you."

His warm lips descended once again to press hungrily against hers. His caress strayed to her cheek, then moved slowly toward her neck.

Toward her right ear. Oh, no! She could feel his soft lips brushing against her earlobe and his breath warming her skin. He was speaking to her, whispering something. A surge of panic arose within her.

She twisted in his embrace so that he should whisper the lovely things he was undoubtedly telling her into the ear with which she could appreciate them.

The lovely sensation of his breath against her neck ceased. Lord Merritt was waiting for a reply. Yet, how could she respond when she had no idea what he had said?

Well, given the circumstances, she had *some* idea. But suppose she was wrong? She wouldn't want to be thought presumptuous!

She felt him repeat his words. Still she dared make no reply.

From the manner in which he wore his clothing, in the very posture in which he held his personage, by the contempt in which he held the dilapidated Penderrick Keep, Rosamunde knew that, for Lord Merritt, everything must be perfect.

She had seen the strange look on his face when she had missed Mr. Whitlaw's remarks that one visit. How could she tell him the truth of her affliction and risk his censure and disapproval now that it was apparent he had some tender feelings for her?

"Rosamunde?" Lord Merritt said sharply. He held her back and searched her eyes. His clear blue eyes showed puzzlement and hurt. "I don't understand. I thought you . . ."

"You thought I could hear you?" she asked.

"No. I thought you . . ."

Unable to wait for his questions regarding her behavior, Rosamunde plunged ahead with the tale of the childhood mishap which had rendered her deaf in one ear.

"I have never told anyone—except Uncle Peg," she admitted as she finished. Silently, she sat staring at the tips of her shoes, waiting for his inevitable rejection.

"I see," Lord Merritt said, rubbing his chin.

From under lowered lids, Rosamunde affectionately watched his familiar gesture. A small knot tightened within her breast as she realized this most probably was the last time he would allow her that sight.

Suddenly Lord Merritt drew her closer to him.

"You truly did not hear a word I said when I whispered in that ear?" he asked, gently reaching up to trace the fine outline of the ridges of her ear with his finger.

Unwilling to move her head lest it break the tender contact with him, she simply said a tiny, "No."

"Then I shall simply have to repeat myself."

Lord Merritt gazed intently into Rosamunde's eyes. Slowly, gently, he moved his hand from her ear to cradle her cheek, then cup her chin in his hand. He bent closer to her and kissed her softly upon the lips. Then he leisurely meandered across her cheek to her left ear, where he bestowed another tender kiss.

Then he whispered, "Rosamunde, I love you."

"Oh, Lord Merritt," she barely whispered.

"Lawrence," he corrected. Then he grinned at her. "I trust you heard me that time."

Rosamunde moved her lips several times before she could actually make a coherent sound. "I know I heard you," she said, smiling shyly at him. Then she shook her head. "But I still cannot believe what I heard."

"Is it so difficult to believe that I am in love with you, Rosamunde?" he asked.

"You do not mind my affliction?"

"Affliction? 'Tis no affliction," he declared. "I view it as a veritable blessing."

Rosamunde stared at him, bewildered. "How so?" she asked. Over the years, she had thought many things regarding her deafness in one ear, yet had never regarded it as a blessing. If his lordship had some marvelous new insight upon it, she truly wanted to hear it.

Lord Merritt grinned and studied her with his intensely blue eyes. "I shall not have to worry about other men's insincere flatteries turning your head," he said. "I'm extremely jealous, you know."

She had *never* expected this reaction. "You just . . ."

"You still do not believe me?" he asked. "Then I shall simply have to make myself more convincing."

This time, he seized her and drew her roughly to him. Enveloping her in his arms, he kissed her passionately. His lips pressed against hers, hard yet not harsh, demanding yet not violating. His murmurs of love turned into deep sounds of his urgency for her.

Then, slowly yet firmly, he pulled back from her. His blue eyes were tightly closed, as if he were concentrating all his inner strengths to maintain his self-control. He emitted a deep, shuddering breath.

"Now do you believe that I love you?" he asked. "And, in whatever time may be left to us in this wretched place, I intend to tell you again and again just how much I love you."

"Oh, Lawrence," she said, still quite breathless. She entwined her arms about his neck. "I love you, too."

"Now hear this!" Sir Polly squawked. "Dead men tell no tales. Augustus Wickes. Full fathom down."

Rosamunde and Lord Merritt, their heads still so close they were touching, turned to face the noisy parrot.

"Dead men tell no tales," Sir Polly repeated. "Augustus Wickes. Full fathom down."

"He has never said that before," Rosamunde said.

"Never?"

Rosamunde shook her head.

"What could have prompted him . . . ?"

"I love you," Rosamunde said.

"I love you, too, my dear," Lord Merritt responded, "but right now, we must discover what has prompted Sir Polly to . . ."

"I love you, you beetle-headed lout!" she exclaimed.

"See here, Rosamunde," Lord Merritt complained. "There is no reason for such temper."

"Do you not understand?" she attempted to explain over Sir Polly's loud and repetitious chatter. "You know nothing of parrots. A word or a phrase can prompt them to say things. He has never said this before, therefore, it must be something which he has not heard before."

"Such as?"

"Such as 'I love you,'" Rosamunde answered.

"But *I* said 'I love you' several times, as a matter of fact, and Sir Polly did not speak then."

"But I did not respond, Lawrence," she said. "It took both of us."

Lord Merritt at last began to smile his comprehension. Rosamunde was relieved that his lordship was not as dense as he had at first appeared. What a horror for their children if he were!

"I'd venture to say that, aboard ship, there are few men and women responding to each other with such terms of endearment," Rosamunde said. "'I love you' would be something the pirate captain might teach his pet to respond to without fear of being easily discovered."

"Then Sir Polly is telling us the location of the treasure!"

Rosamunde and Lord Merritt sat quietly holding each other, barely breathing lest they miss a single word Sir Polly said. Not once did he pause or change his soliloquy.

"Who is Augustus Wickes?" Lord Merritt whispered. "What has he to do with the treasure?"

"If we could get out of this mine, we could find him."

"Unless he is dead," Lord Merritt reminded her. "Dead men tell no tales."

"He *is* dead," she answered. "Augustus Wickes was Uncle Peg's grandfather, my great-grandfather. But he died when Uncle Peg was just a boy. How could he have the treasure?"

Lord Merritt's blue eyes fairly sparkled with humor and delight. In a sorry imitation of Uncle Peg, he declared, "Do ye be the kin of a pirate and not know a fathom be six feet down?"

"In water, yes."

"And what other measurement would a seafaring man use?"

Rosamunde and Lord Merritt stared at each other with growing realization.

Breathlessly, Rosamunde began, "They buried the treasure . . ."

"In his grave," he finished for her.

Lord Merritt slowly disentangled himself from Rosamunde. He examined the wall he had tried unsuccessfully to scale before.

"Oh, Lawrence, don't," she pleaded. "In your search for that blasted treasure, you'll only injure yourself again—or kill us both in the bargain."

"Oh, no. Before I had only the faint hope of restoring my mother's honor," Lord Merritt said. "But that was in the past. Now I know you love me as I love you. Now I have a future to plan for—a future with you. This time I *will* succeed—for the sake of the *two* most important women in my life."

Rosamunde held her breath as she watched him dig into the wall. She coughed and brushed from her face the dirt which continually cascaded down the wall as, inch by inch, he moved slowly toward the top.

A face appeared suddenly, looming over the edge. Lord Merritt started backward, almost falling.

"Blast it all, Childers!" he exclaimed, grasping at a clump of grass on the crumbling side for purchase. "Must you sneak up upon a man like that when he's trying to climb out of a mine shaft?"

"How do you think I feel?" John Childers responded. "I surely was not expecting to look into a hole and find your lordship popping out like a ferret."

"Unlike a ferret, I could use a bit of assistance to get out. If you'd be so good, Childers?" Lord Merritt requested.

Childers firmly grasped Lord Merritt's hand and hauled him up.

Rosamunde gathered up Lord Merritt's jacket and rapier. She managed to coax a still-chattering Sir Polly back onto her shoulder before ascending the ladder Lord Merritt and Childers sent back down to her.

"Who *are* you?" Rosamunde demanded of the rotund man when she reached the top. "How did you find us?"

She still did not know who the man was, nor if she could trust him. But he had gotten them out of that miserable mine shaft, and for that she would always be grateful to him.

Bowing to her, he answered, "John Childers, miss. Sorry to have taken so long. I had to be certain Raikes and Gidley were gone."

"You followed them here?" Lord Merritt asked.

"No. I followed *you* here."

"How did you know where we were?" Rosamunde asked.

"I've been following you since you left the inn," he replied with a small chuckle.

"But you left by the front," Rosamunde said. "We left by the back."

"If I were not extremely good at following people unnoticed, I would be dead by now," Childers explained.

But Rosamunde was still bewildered. "You are no pirate. Are you, then, a spy?"

"From time to time, I've done my duty by the Crown," he answered.

"Why are you following Raikes and Gidley—and us?" Lord Merritt demanded.

"My father was the constable here when the *Dauntless* and *Halverton* sank," Childers said. "I was just a lad then, but how well I remember my mother taking in and caring for the lone survivor, a boy not much older than myself."

"Uncle Peg," Rosamunde said.

"I remember Dudley laying deathly ill in our spare bedchamber and raving about stolen treasure," Childers continued. "The adults said he was delirious with fever, and paid him no mind. But I believed him. And when the news came of the loss of the Penderrick fortune, I put two and two together . . ."

"And I suppose you've come to claim the treasure, too," Lord Merritt said.

"Not for myself, m'lord," Childers disclaimed. "Just as my father always did his duty by the law, I have made it mine to see the treasure returned to its rightful owner."

"I never did think you had the look of a pirate, Mr. Childers," Lord Merritt said.

"Then we truly can trust you?" Rosamunde asked. "You will help us?"

"Oh, indeed, miss." Childers nodded.

A loud crack reverberated through the air. Childers' head slumped to his chest and he fell forward. Rosamunde dropped Lord Merritt's jacket and the ancient rapier and bent over the unconscious man.

Raikes, a smoking pistol in his hand, walked toward them, followed by the hulking form of Gidley.

Before she could rise and flee, Raikes seized her by the wrist and began pulling her along.

"Lawrence," she cried to him for help. But Lord Merritt was quite occupied already. The long knife in Gidley's hand glinted in the lantern light as he menaced it toward his lordship's heart.

Rosamunde's heart pounded in her throat so hard that she could not even cry out. How could fate be so unkind as to allow her to find the man she loved only to see him cruelly dispatched, all within an hour's time!

Yet, to her immense relief, Lord Merritt dodged the deadly blade again and again. How much longer could he continue to be so fortunate?

The rapier! If only he had the rapier! Rosamunde silently wailed.

"The coat," she cried to him. " 'Tis under your coat!"

She doubted he could hear her as she was pulled inexorably along by Raikes. She struggled against his grasp, but could not shake herself free.

Sir Polly flapped his wings and clutched Rosamunde's shoulder more tightly. All the while, he continued to repeat, "Dead men tell no tales. Augustus Wickes. Full fathom down."

"Oh, do be quiet, Sir Polly!" she exclaimed.

" 'Tis no use," Raikes said with a deep chuckle. "I heard him, and now I, too, know where to look."

As he pulled her along, Rosamunde lamented to herself, 'All this time trying to make Sir Polly reveal the location of the treasure, and now, in front of the very people we must keep from the treasure, *now* I cannot shut him up!'

The sky was just beginning to lighten over Penzance Harbor as Raikes and Rosamunde reached the lonely graveyard. He grabbed a shovel from the sexton's shed.

"Show me where it is!" he commanded.

She was more concerned with her beloved Lawrence, left at the mercy of that silent ogre Gidley, than she could ever be concerned with the location of mere money.

"I . . . I don't remember," Rosamunde said hesitantly.

" 'Tis hard to remember where one's great-grandfather is buried. We visit so infrequently . . ."

Raikes tightened his grip on her wrist. His face came so close to hers she could even smell his rotting teeth.

"Ye'll be buried near him if ye don't be remembering quick-like."

She pressed her lips together and ordered her stomach to remain calm. She'd not lose her aplomb—nor her dinner—in front of this scoundrel!

"Under the circumstances, you can hardly blame me for being rather befuddled," she told him haughtily, and slowly, trying to play for more time. "Just give me a moment to think."

"Ye'll think better on yer feet," he said. Raikes tugged her about the cemetery, winding his way among the graves.

She dragged her feet and resisted with every step. He fidgeted with the pistol in his hand and continually glanced about him. Rosamunde could tell he was becoming increasingly impatient. The sun was nearly up. If they did not retrieve the treasure soon, doubtless more than a few people would be inquiring as to precisely why Miss Rosamunde Wickes and a strange old pirate were digging up the village cemetery.

If she could only keep Raikes waiting, delay him just a little longer. Perhaps the constable would come by—or even Mr. Shelby. Perhaps Childers had not been killed and would find her. Perhaps her own dear Lawrence would survive the murderous Gidley and come to her rescue.

"Ah! There it be!" Raikes exclaimed as he pulled her to a halt in front of the small, weathered tombstone. "Augustus Wickes, eh?" He chuckled. "Clever old bilge rat, to bury the treasure here. 'Twas a driving rain all that night. He turned the sod carefully, buried the chest, and covered it over again just as carefully. The rain washed the extra dirt away and settled in the new digging, with nary a soul the wiser." He nodded. "Aye. That would be how he did it."

"Let me go, now," Rosamunde pleaded. "You know where the treasure is. You don't need me any longer."

Raikes shook his head. "Ye be just a bit of insurance for an old pirate." He pushed the shovel at her and ordered, "Dig."

Rosamunde glared from Raikes to the shovel and back again with as much disdain as she could manage.

"You want *me* to dig?" she repeated incredulously. "I thought you intended to retrieve this treasure some time this year."

"I can't have ye running off while me back is turned."

"Well . . . well, I can't just go digging up the cemetery," Rosamunde protested, desperate for any reason that would prolong the wait. "I really should ask the vicar first, or at least the sexton."

Did Raikes grimace? she wondered. Mr. Shelby was surely not dangerous. The worst thing the Silent Vicar could do was bore a person to death.

"We won't be needing the vicar," Raikes insisted. "At any rate, no one's seen the lubber all day . . . at least that's the scuttlebutt."

'Probably hiding under his bed,' Rosamunde thought, then felt rather guilty about such an unkind observation. Well, considering the circumstances, she might be forgiven that *one* uncharitable thought.

Rosamunde racked her brain for another excuse. But her mind was too full of worry for Lord Merritt to function properly.

"Dig!"

She had no alternative but to begin.

Sir Polly deserted her to perch upon a nearby tombstone.

Rosamunde was accustomed to housework. She was even accustomed to assisting her father with some of his gardening, when he permitted anyone near his precious flowers. But she was in no manner prepared to dig in the long-undisturbed soil for any length of time.

She stopped several times to catch her breath, but Raikes

always waved the pistol at her, providing an irresistible incentive to continue.

"If you do not let me rest, I shall be dead before we reach six feet down," she finally told him.

"Well, then, if ye do, we won't be needing to dig ye a grave, will we?"

Rosamunde resumed her digging.

Suddenly, a little less than three feet down, her shovel hit something.

"Oh, merciful heavens, let it be the blasted chest!" Rosamunde prayed aloud.

Raikes tucked the pistol into his belt and jumped down into the hole. Heedless of Rosamunde, he finished unearthing his prize and pulled the small wooden chest out. It was bound with strips of leather, with brass studs and brass handles on either side. A thick, rusty chain was double-wrapped about it and secured with a large, rusted lock.

Raikes jammed the point of the shovel into the hasp. The corroded metal split in two.

He threw back the chains and lifted the lid. The shining coins sparkled in the first rays of the dawn. Raikes began to chuckle as he ran his fingers through the gold coins.

Rosamunde took advantage of his preoccupation with the treasure to climb out of the shallow hole. Sir Polly once again resumed her perch on her shoulder.

"So, lass," Raikes said as he rose from his concentration on the long-sought treasure. "I do thank ye for yer cooperation in the matter. 'Tis a pity a lass as pretty as yerself has outlived her usefulness."

"What do you mean?" she asked. Her knees began to shake and her body tensed. She knew precisely what he meant.

'Oh, where is Lawrence?' she wondered. He *would*—he must—arrive in time, she tried to reassure herself. She refused even to consider the possibility that he might already be dead. Yet, she knew that if Lawrence were dead at the hands of the hideous Gidley, she would not want to continue living the rest of her life without him.

"I cannot have ye identifying me to the authorities. There's a ship leaves Penzance at dawn for the port o' New York, and I'll be aboard her."

"What of Gidley?" she asked. She didn't care a fig about Gidley, but if the conversation prolonged her life just long enough for Lord Merritt, Lawrence, to arrive, Gidley would have served his purpose.

Raikes chuckled again. "Oh, Gidley'll have his share o' the treasure, if he can catch me."

"You'd cheat your own partner?" she asked. "Why, you *are* despicable."

"More so than ye'll ever know," Raikes replied.

Slowly, he lifted the pistol and pointed it directly at her head.

Oh, she was done for now!

"No quarter! No prisoners!" Sir Polly cried.

He flew into Raikes' face, his long talons clawing, and his sharp, hooked beak pecking at the hands which Raikes raised to protect his eyes.

Rosamunde dove for the fallen pistol.

"Oh, we'll take prisoners," John Childers' voice assured Sir Polly.

Although she was not without some feeling of relief at seeing John Childers still alive, it was Lord Merritt she sought.

She left the pistol where it had fallen. Let Childers retrieve it—that was his job anyway. Lord Merritt was running toward her and that was the only thing she truly saw.

"Oh, Lawrence! Thank God, you're all right!" she murmured as she rushed into the safety of his embrace. "I was so afraid Gidley would kill you."

"I have survived being trapped in a mine shaft, and even being inundated by Fickle and all his kin," Lord Merritt said, holding her close. "You did not think a little thing like Gidley would prevent me from coming to you."

"A *little* thing!" she demanded, drawing back to gaze into his eyes. She smiled at him with immense relief. She smoothed her hand over his cheek and into his rumpled hair. "How did you escape?"

"I heard you call out," he explained. "When I tried to retrieve the rapier, I threw the coat up into Gidley's face. He could not see where he was going and fell to his death in the mine shaft."

"Oh, how horrid!" Rosamunde shuddered. "Even for Gidley."

Lord Merritt held her more closely to him, cradling her against him, the better to blot out her memories of this horrid night.

Suddenly he noticed the chest at Raikes' feet.

"You found it!" he exclaimed. He squeezed her tightly in his excitement. Then he held her out from him to gaze, smiling, into her eyes. "You truly found it!"

"Indeed, we have found your treasure, at last."

"But 'tis not mine."

"After all we have just been through to retrieve this blasted thing!" she exclaimed. "Are you telling me now you do not want it?"

" 'Tis no longer mine," he said. " 'Twas found on property belonging to the Wickes family, and by rights it belongs to you."

"My family will not take your treasure a second time," Rosamunde protested.

Lord Merritt released one arm from about Rosamunde just long enough to stroke his chin. "Then I see no other alternative. I propose we share the fortune."

"Share it?"

"Indeed," Lord Merritt replied with a solemn nod. "I believe a husband and wife should share everything."

"M'lord," Raikes called from over top Childers' watchful form. "Begging yer lordship's pardon, but we had a deal. A share o' the treasure when it be found. 'Tis only fair, m'lord."

Rosamunde glared angrily at the old pirate. "Fair? You have the audacity to cry 'fair'?"

Lord Merritt laid a calming hand on her arm. "We did indeed strike a bargain."

Lord Merritt released Rosamunde and strode to the open chest and began to reach inside.

"No!" Rosamunde declared, rushing to Lord Merritt's side to stop him. "Raikes may have fulfilled *your* part of the bargain, but he has not yet fulfilled *mine*."

She turned upon Raikes and glared at him. "There'll be no share of the treasure until you tell me. Where is Mary Ann?"

Raikes frowned and pursed his lips. He shifted from one foot to the other and glanced about. At last, he admitted, "I don't have her. 'Twas that wretched little parson took her from us."

"Mr. Shelby?" Lord Merritt asked. "Oh, come now. I find that extremely difficult to believe."

"I swear on me mother's grave," Raikes vowed. "If I knew who she was."

Rosamunde turned to Lord Merritt. "Oh, however shall we find her now?"

"Mr. Shelby has taken Mary Ann home," his lordship assured her. "Undoubtedly."

"Oh, undoubtedly," Raikes confirmed.

Lord Merritt reached into the chest and scooped up a handful of coins. He trickled them into Raikes' outstretched hand.

"Yer a man o' yer word, m'lord," Raikes said, eyeing the pile of coins appreciatively. "And I do thank ye. As I understand, Newgate be rather inhospitable to one ill-equipped to pay for one's necessaries there."

=SIXTEEN=

"You have found the treasure!" Mrs. Wickes exclaimed when Rosamunde and Lord Merritt entered Eglantine Cottage late that morning. She made no mention of Rosamunde's bedraggled gown and dirt-sprinkled hair, nor of Lord Merritt's injured arm.

In fact, she completely bypassed Rosamunde and Lord Merritt and made straight for the heavy chest his lordship held.

Neither did it seem to bother her that Mary Ann and the vicar had not been seen since yesterday afternoon. She was much too busy running her hands through the deep pile of coins.

"Oh, bravo, old man!" Roger exclaimed. "So you finally found it."

He attempted to join Mrs. Wickes in her admiration of the newly found treasure, but she pushed him away.

"Sir Polly told us where to find it," Lord Merritt corrected.

"We searched so long, we put up with so much for that wretched bird's sake, and then he tells *you*!" Mrs. Wickes lamented. "What was the clue?"

Lord Merritt shrugged his broad shoulders evasively. "Suddenly he just started talking. He told us where to dig. Unfortunately, Raikes and Gidley heard as well."

"Were it not for Sir Polly's bravery, I should be dead," Rosamunde said. She recounted her feathered companion's brave act that had saved her life.

Mrs. Wickes did manage to disengage herself from the treasure long enough to say, "Why, what a marvelous bird Sir Polly is, too!"

"Keel haul the bilious doxy!" Sir Polly replied, obviously immune to her insincere flatteries.

"A pity you could not find Mary Ann, too," Mr. Wickes commented. "I do hope she's safe."

"Indeed, she is," replied Mr. Shelby as he and Mary Ann boldly strode into the sitting room.

"Oh, Mary Ann! You had no idea how worried I was!" Rosamunde exclaimed, rushing to her stepsister. She enfolded her in her arms, quite expecting the timid girl to swoon.

"I'm quite undamaged," Mary Ann replied. She disentangled herself from Rosamunde's embrace and again clasped Mr. Shelby's hand.

"Mary Ann!" Mrs. Wickes declared, at last deigning to rise from her adoration of the treasure. "Where have you been? Lord Merritt has been looking all over for you."

"Well, he didn't find me, did he?" Mary Ann replied.

Rosamunde was exceedingly surprised. Considering the ordeal through which the girl had just gone, Mary Ann appeared extraordinarily calm—quite a change, indeed.

"Rosamunde, I lay the blame for all this directly at your feet, " Mrs. Wickes accused. "We have spoken before regarding certain persons rescuing certain other persons and what the consequences thereof might be. Yet, still you persisted in assisting Lord Merritt in finding the treasure and not Mary Ann."

"However did you manage to escape?" Rosamunde asked her stepsister.

"And what are you doing with Mr. Shelby?" Mrs. Wickes demanded, eyeing that gentleman suspiciously.

"Mr. Shelby rescued me," Mary Ann announced.

"Oh, Mary Ann is quite brave," Mr. Shelby said, gazing adoringly down into her blue eyes.

"Oh, no, Josiah!" Mary Ann exclaimed, as she, too,

gazed adoringly into Mr. Shelby's drooping brown eyes. " 'Tis *you* who are brave."

"Is it true?" Rosamunde demanded. "Did Mr. Shelby indeed rescue you?"

"Indeed. We've discovered that Josiah has physical talents heretofore unrecognized," Mary Ann answered for him.

"I could not allow anything to happen to my beloved Mary Ann," Mr. Shelby modestly admitted.

"Oh, hush, Mr. Shelby," Mrs. Wickes declared. "What will Lord Merritt think?"

Even now, would Stepmama *never* make an end of it? Rosamunde lamented. Well, if Mary Ann could be brave, she supposed she could, too.

"Stepmama, do give it up," Rosamunde declared. "Can you not see, even now, how things truly are?"

Mrs. Wickes, quite speechless for perhaps the first time, merely stared at both Mary Ann and Rosamunde.

"I hope his lordship will wish us happy," Mr. Shelby replied with a smile.

Mrs. Wickes stared at her daughter and the vicar and began to groan. She finally collapsed onto the sofa as she realized what was transpiring.

"Oh, Mary Ann, after all my efforts, you cannot mean . . ."

"Indeed, I do mean to marry your daughter. I have obtained a special license," Mr. Shelby explained. "We intend to be married tomorrow by my uncle, the archbishop."

Mrs. Wickes suddenly ceased her lamentations and sat upright upon the sofa.

"Archbishop?" she repeated, staring at Mr. Shelby. A wide smile began to spread across her face. "Your uncle, the archbishop?"

"My father's younger brother," Mr. Shelby said. "His older brother is Lord Shelbourne."

Mrs. Wickes drew in a great gasp of air. "Oh, merciful

heavens! I should have known . . . And the Widow Camberton, that sly boots, never once mentioned . . ." she
murmured to herself. "Why, dear Mr. Shelby!" Mrs.
Wickes suddenly smiled ingratiatingly at him. "You never
told us you had such highly placed family."

"You never bothered to ask," he replied coolly. "I
suppose as long as you considered me good enough only for
a stepdaughter, it did not much signify. Now that I am to
wed your daughter, the possibility of my following in my
uncle's footsteps seems much more pertinent."

"Why, Mr. Shelby, how can you think that?" Mrs.
Wickes asked with a great gulp as she swallowed her pride.
"I always did think you a capital fellow."

"To be sure."

"At any rate, must the wedding be so soon?" she asked.
She eyed the treasure appreciatively. "After all, now that
we can afford it, Mr. Wickes and I would so like to hold a
festive celebration. Mary Ann needs a new frock. I should
dearly love a new carpet, perhaps new wallpapers."

"Oh, no, Mama," Mary Ann said. "There is no time for
all that."

Mrs. Wickes sank back against the sofa cushions again.
"Oh, *never* tell me this has been going on longer than I
suspected! *Never* tell me you are—oh, dare I say it?—
enceinte!"

"Mama! Of course not!" Mary Ann declared, frowning
with injured pride. Mr. Shelby flushed deeply.

"Then I fail to see why you cannot comply with a fond
mother's wishes for her only daughter."

"Because Josiah and I shall be leaving in a month's time
for the missions of India," Mary Ann explained.

"India!" Mrs. Wickes cried, placing a shaking hand to
her ample breast. "Among the heathen? Among the—why,
I shudder to even mention—the cannibals!"

"Cannibals? Do not be ridiculous, Mama," Mary Ann
scoffed. "The Hindu eat only vegetables. I have nothing to
fear from them."

Rosamunde grinned at her stepsister. "I should say you would not fear anything from anyone."

Mary Ann held more tightly to Mr. Shelby's hand. "Not with Josiah at my side."

'Oh, merciful heavens!' Rosamunde silently wailed. 'If this is an example of the transformed Mary Ann and Josiah, I am heartily relieved that those two will be leaving soon.'

"No grand wedding. No gown of silk and satin and imported lace. No sumptuous wedding breakfast," Mrs. Wickes lamented, looking about the dilapidated sitting room of the dreary dilapidated little cottage in which she had spent so much time. "Not even a new carpet for the sitting room."

Suddenly Mrs. Wickes turned to her daughter and frowned. "Oh, Mary Ann," she scolded, "however could you have been so inconsiderate when deciding upon your marriage?"

Mary Ann merely shrugged off her mother's complaints and gazed adoringly into Mr. Shelby's eyes.

"I should not feel too badly if I were you, Mrs. Wickes," Lord Merritt said comfortingly.

"Well, my lord, 'tis not *your only* daughter who is marrying without even giving you time to . . ."

"There *will* be another wedding in the Wickes family," he interrupted her complaint.

"Well," Mrs. Wickes said with a sigh, "I suppose, someday, there is the barest chance that Rosamunde might find someone who does not mind her age . . ."

"She *has* found someone, Mrs. Wickes," Lord Merritt said, placing his arm firmly about Rosamunde's waist. "And I have found more than just the Penderrick treasure. With your kind permission—well, even without it— Rosamunde and I intend to be married."

"Rosamunde! And your lordship?" Mrs. Wickes said, as if to clarify the match in her mind. "My lord, I realize you must be quite shocked by Mary Ann's marrying the vicar instead of you, but you needn't marry Rosamunde just to soothe your unrequited—"

Lord Merritt laughed. "Mary Ann is a lovely young woman, Mrs. Wickes, but I assure you, my heart belongs only to Rosamunde."

His lordship then turned to Mr. Wickes. "Will you give your consent, sir?"

"Indeed! And my blessing!" Mr. Wickes exclaimed.

"How marvelous!" Mrs. Wickes, now quite recovered, began chattering. "How fortunate can a mother be to have one daughter married to Lord Shelbourne's nephew and another daughter wed to the Viscount Merritt? A mother's dream come true!"

Rosamunde merely bit her tongue and smiled at Stepmama. Of course, her *only* daughter had been marrying Mr. Shelby, until the *other one* had suddenly become the betrothed of Lord Merritt—and became her daughter, too.

"Oh, Rosamunde, I do hope you intend to wait longer than Mary Ann," Mrs. Wickes said. "We've such plans to make for you."

"Lord Merritt and I have not yet discussed our immediate plans," Rosamunde said, glancing shyly at his lordship. Indeed, they had been so preoccupied with present dangers that plans for the future, which at that point seemed quite uncertain, had never arisen.

Lord Merritt smiled and drew Rosamunde closer to him.

"Mrs. Wickes, you may make whatever plans please you," his lordship said. "For the moment, however, I think Miss Bellows' and Mr. Shelby's plans take precedence."

"Oh, well, I suppose so," Mrs. Wickes replied. Rosamunde could plainly see that Mary Ann and Mr. Shelby's hasty preparations paled before the shameless extravagance which Mrs. Wickes was contemplating for the future Lady Merritt.

"While you are formulating those plans," Lord Merritt said, "Miss Wickes and I have some plans of our own to make."

His lordship wrapped his arm about Rosamunde's shoulder and led her out the door to the terrace. They stepped around the few shrubs Mr. Wickes had not yet had time to replant. They wandered down to the cliffs at the end of the garden which overlooked the sea.

Sheltered in the small arbor, Lord Merritt turned Rosamunde to face him. Slowly, he drew her to him until she pressed against his lean body. He did not need to raise her face to his, as she already looked up into his eyes.

How could a man resist her? Why should he; he asked himself. She was his, with nothing ever again to come between them. Still, he clutched her to him as if afraid to let her go. He kissed her, slowly at first, lingering, savoring the sweet flavor of her mouth. As she pressed herself closer to him and twisted her fingers through his hair, his kiss became more fierce.

Slowly, he raised his lips from hers, yet still held her tightly to him.

"You and I have some plans to make, Rosamunde," he said.

"I scarcely know what to think or say, Lawrence," she answered him. "When I was a child, I planned on having great adventures in faraway places, like Uncle Peg. I never did, so, eventually, I stopped dreaming of adventure. Of late, I rather supposed I should end my days a lonely spinster at Eglantine Cottage."

"How inconsiderate of me to have ruined your plans!" Lord Merritt said.

"I think I shall be able to find it in my heart to forgive you," she assured him.

"Then the first thing you need to do is have a wedding gown made, one with yards and yards of silk and French lace, just the type of gown which would look perfect in the chapel of Penderrick Keep."

She frowned and looked at him askance. "But, Lawrence, I thought you said you were planning to sell Penderrick Keep as soon as possible."

"Ah well, as you can see, sometimes the best-laid plans

can go awry," he told her. "As Fickle and his bizarre family tidied up the Keep, I began to have second thoughts. 'Twas not such a dreadful place after all. But what truly changed my mind was when I went there with you."

Rosamunde watched him, clearly bewildered.

"I saw what a wonderful place Penderrick Keep could be for raising children," he explained. "Lots of children—*our* children."

"Lots of children?" Rosamunde repeated cautiously.

"Our children," Lord Merritt assured her.

He drew her closer to him. Once again his silver-blue eyes were a mirror of fiery passion. He moved his hand gently up and down her arms. Then, slowly, reverently, his hand brushed against the roundness of her breast to cup it tenderly in his hand.

"*Our* children, Rosamunde," he repeated breathlessly.

He kissed her once, then released her and drew back a step.

"I know you have always wanted a life of adventure, Rosamunde," he said. "And I am heartily sorry that the life which I offer you will not be as exciting as the life which Mr. Shelby offers Mary Ann. During the Season, and the Little Season should you so choose, we will stay at Merritt House in placid Cavendish Square and attend the usual round of tedious balls and soirees and court functions. We can winter at quiet Edmonston Hall or isolated Penderrick Keep. We can summer at Brighton or Bath. Nothing very exciting at either of those places, I can assure you."

Rosamunde entwined her arms about his neck and drew his face down close to hers. She placed a soft kiss at the corner of his mouth and whispered, "Oh, I think you might be able to devise *something* which would excite me."

Lord Merritt's icy blue eyes turned to fire. He held her tightly to him once again.

"Oh, Rosamunde," he promised. "I shall do my best."

"Oh, Lawrence," she responded. "You have made a wonderful start."